I0668571

Last Hope

The Billionaires' Club Series: Book 7

AE Moran

The Invisible Publishing Company

The Billionaires' Club Series

Contents

Chapter 1:
McKenna

"The billionaires are here, Mr. Metcalf!" I call through the office door.

Jackson Metcalf groans behind his desk. "When are you ever going to stop calling me that, McKenna? You've been working for me for six years. I think you can call me by my first name."

I laugh at him. "I could never do that—and I think you can stop asking. I'm not going to call you by your first name. That wouldn't be appropriate. You're my boss. You'll always be Mr. Metcalf to me."

"What if I order you to do it? Would you do it then?"

I can't help but laugh and my cheeks color. "Probably not. Do you need anything else for the conference room—tea, coffee, donuts...."

Now it's his turn to laugh. He stands up from behind the desk and his eyes twinkle as he crosses the room toward me. His size dwarfs me and he always walks straight and fast whenever he goes anywhere.

He's one of the most hard-driving, hard-working, determined men I've ever met, but he's also one of the sweetest, most caring, and attentive to the people around him. Everyone who works for him adores him.

People who don't work for him sometimes say they're afraid of him. He can be harsh and stern when someone doesn't do what they're supposed to do.

He's never acted that way toward me—probably because I always do my job the way I'm supposed to. I wouldn't want to let him down.

"I think you better keep the donuts for yourself, young lady," he teases. "I haven't eaten one in years and I'm quite certain none of the other billionaires have, either."

I know they haven't which is why I made the joke. I head for the elevator and Jackson follows me out of the office. We meet Dante Helme, Kevin Drake, and Rory Kahn coming out of the elevator together.

That's one thing I can say about the men in The Billionaires' Club. They all take excellent care of themselves. None of them is as big and hulking as Jackson. He's almost as tall as Judah Hayes and much broader in the shoulders.

Each of them is kind, considerate, and they all treat employees well, including other people's employees. Kevin smiles at me. "Hello, McKenna. You look like you're blooming."

I blush at him. "You're going to give a girl ideas, Mr. Drake. Come right this way, gentlemen. Mr. Metcalf is....."

"I'm right here," Jackson replies from behind me.

He goes through the group shaking hands with the other billionaires. They're all good friends. They clap each other on their shoulders and enter the conference room together. That's my cue to disappear.

I go back to my desk and finish drawing up Jackson's schedule for next month. It's a busy month because he has a bunch of meetings with the accounting departments of all his many companies to do their annual financial audits and reviews.

I don't think anything of Jackson's meeting with the other billionaires. They're in there planning their next club networking conference and a few other events. This meeting is nothing serious.

I'm just backing up his schedule and syncing it to all his devices when I get a text from him asking me to bring him the information we have on four new companies he's considering acquiring.

I stop what I'm doing, get the paperwork, and take it into the conference room. The billionaires aren't talking about club events anymore. They're talking business. It always happens this way. They can't help themselves.

I hand the paperwork to Jackson planning to slip out unseen. "Could you please stick around for a minute, McKenna?" Jackson asks. "Kevin wants to schedule a few other meetings for next month."

"Don't you already have enough going on next month?" I ask. "Can't you wait until Christmas at the earliest?"

All four men burst out laughing. "I really wish I could," Kevin replies.

I take out my phone and use my stylus to navigate to the schedule I just spent so much time arranging. "When do you want to schedule them?"

I hear the four men talking to me and to each other, but right then, a wave of cold, blackness grips me all over. I can't even raise my eyes from my phone. I feel myself falling....falling....

I hear Jackson yelling my name, but he sounds like he's far away. He bends over me on the floor. Rory stands right behind Jackson. Rory is on the phone with someone talking fast.

I hover somewhere between consciousness and unconsciousness. I can't feel anything except this cold darkness creeping over me.

I barely feel hands touching my body. I must really have passed out because I wake up in the back of an ambulance on my way to the hospital. Three medics work over me doing something or other.

I keep my eyes shut while they take me inside. They leave me alone for a while. Doctors and nurses keep coming around to check on me. I'm too out of it even to think straight.

I finally swim back to consciousness lying in a regular hospital bed. I'm alone....except for Jackson sitting in the chair next to my bed.

I try to sit up and swallow down the sting of bile in my throat. "What are you....where's the.....I have to...."

He jumps out of his chair and comes to my bedside. "Don't try to sit up. You're going to need a lot of rest from now on."

"What are you talking about?" I look around me everywhere. "What are you doing here? You have a business to run."

"I had to make sure you were all right." He pats my hand.

He's always been super kind and affectionate toward me, but he always keeps it professional. He would never cross a line with anyone—ever. He doesn't do that kind of thing.

"It took the doctors ages to figure out what was wrong with you," he tells me.

I frown at him and then I remember. My eyes dart to the clock on the wall. "I have to get out of here. I've been in here too long already."

I start to throw back the sheets and blankets that cover me. I'm still fully clothed.

"You can't do that." Jackson tries to push me back down. "Sweet ie.....I didn't want to be the one to tell you this, but....."

My eyes shoot up to him. "What's wrong?"

"You......you have leukemia. The doctors say.....well, they don't know how long you have....They say it's advancing more rapidly than they're used to seeing....they think...."

I overreact and knock his hand off my shoulder. "Get out of my way, Mr. Metcalf. I have to go."

"You can't. You could collapse again. You could put yourself in danger."

I glare at him and push him away even harder. "I said get out of my way. I'm leaving."

He steps back. I don't want to see his features trembling with concern and heartfelt anguish. This is a disaster.

He follows me on the way to the door. I already feel weak and unsteady just from standing up.

"You don't have to do this alone," he tells me from behind. "Let me help you. I can help you pay for treatment. Let me do something to help you. Come on, McKenna."

I stop in front of the nurses' station and tell them to give me my release paperwork. "You shouldn't be here, Mr. Metcalf," I tell him over my shoulder while I sign the documents. "Just go back to your business or whatever it is you want to do. This doesn't concern you."

"You concern me," he insists. "Don't push me away when you need my help."

"I don't need anything from you. Just leave me alone."

I storm out of the hospital and stop on the sidewalk outside. I don't have my car here. It's back in the parking lot outside the Metcalf Mining Industries office building where I work.

I can't afford to take a cab to go pick up my car. I just have to walk it even though it's miles away.

I feel how weak I am. How can I have leukemia? How come no one picked it up before now—and how did it come on so fast?

I don't even want to think about it. I get into my car and drive across town to my children's school. The school has an afterschool daycare program for people who have to work. My kids stay there each afternoon until I come to pick them up.

I get there just at the right time—as if I've been at work all day instead of in the hospital. I can't afford the bill for that, either—but I guess I won't have that problem when I'm dead.

My kids rush into my arms and hug me. "Mom!" my thirteen-year-old daughter Evie exclaims. "You won't believe the picture I drew! Come and look!"

She pulls me over to the table. My eleven-year-old son Alvin wants to show me a skyscraper he built out of popsicle sticks. I feel myself getting emotional while we stand there talking. The teachers are already cleaning up the center for the day. We have to leave soon.

How in the world am I going to tell my children about this? I'm a single parent. I'm all they have.

I finally steer them out of the building. "Let's go home," I tell them. "We can talk all you want once we get there."

I drive them home and start making dinner. The kids talk to me about everything happening at school, all the little dramas with their friends, and every other detail of their lives.

They don't ask me how my day went. They never do. That's my job—to be invisible and make them the most important focal point of our existence.

I sit across from them at the dinner table while they hold a heated debate about the historical and biological accuracy of the *Jurassic Park* films.

Alvin goes on at length about how the dinosaurs would have died out on the island long before the second film ever happened. He says their populations weren't big enough to sustain the genetic variation needed to keep the population going.

He also claims that the same environmental conditions that caused the dinosaurs to go extinct in the first place would eventually wipe out the dinosaurs on the island.

He claims that even a modern-day tropical island close to the equator wouldn't be hot enough or have enough food to keep that many dinosaurs alive.

Evie counters that the cloning experiment never would have worked in the first place and that the whole concept is pure speculative fantasy, so it doesn't matter if the dinosaurs would have survived or not.

Alvin discounts this argument and wants to continue exploring the biological and evolutionary implications. I don't get involved in their discussion.

I have to tell my children the truth eventually, but I don't want to. I just want them to enjoy the time we have left. I don't want to completely crush their hopes by telling them that the love we share can't last.

Chapter 2: Jackson

I frown when I walk into the office and see that McKenna isn't at her desk again this morning. She hasn't come into work since she collapsed and got her leukemia diagnosis.

She also hasn't called in to tell me if she's quitting or not. I wouldn't tolerate this from any other employee, but I can't make a federal case out of it with her—not after what happened at the hospital.

I can't even blame her for pushing me away and turning down my offer to help her. Getting such catastrophic news would do that to anyone.

I just wish I could do something for her even if it's just being there and letting her know I care. I don't want to let this go.

I sit down behind my desk and start working out what I need to do to get ready for my appointments today. Having an assistant do all of this for me is a nice luxury to have, but I can still handle my affairs on my own.

The fact that she isn't here annoys me, though. I can't ignore it. It keeps intruding on whatever I try to concentrate on.

I make up my mind to get to the bottom of this, even if it means she quits and I have to hire another assistant. I have to find out one way or the other so I can move on.

I rearrange a few things and make some time for myself to go see her. I have her address. She lives in a modest apartment in midtown.

I spend the rest of the morning concentrating on work. I can only justify taking time off for this if I stay on top of all my other obligations.

I drive over to her apartment at lunchtime and park outside her building. It isn't the nicest, but she does well for herself on her salary.

I ride the elevator up to her apartment and approach the door. The door stands open and a wall of boxes lines the hallway wall outside.

I stop outside the doorway and look into her apartment. Half a dozen half-full boxes scatter across the living room floor with a whole bunch of stuff from the bookshelves stacked on the floor nearby. She looks like she's in the middle of packing up to move.

McKenna's voice floats through the door from somewhere inside. Then I hear her children yelling back and forth and laughing. They should be in school today—not home with her.

I don't know how to proceed or what this means. I'm still standing there when she comes back into the living room.

She usually wears a business suit to work, but she still looks beautiful in a pair of casual brown slacks and a white T-shirt under an unbuttoned checked shirt with the sleeves rolled up.

A brown elastic hairband holds her wavy, dark brown hair tied in a messy bun with stray locks bouncing around her deep green eyes.

She sees me, straightens up, and her expression goes dark. She's never looked at me like that. She's usually sunny, bubbly, and cheerful.

I scramble for something to say to her. How should I broach the subject to ask if she even still works for me anymore?

Her children rush into the living room just then, surround her, and turn around and see me standing there.

Her son, Alvin, is a lively boy with light reddish-blonde hair, bright blue eyes, and a ton of freckles. He's just starting to shoot up, but he hasn't hit puberty yet.

His sister, Evie, is as tall as McKenna and definitely in puberty now. She's just growing baby breasts and developing her curves. She wears her dark brown hair in a braid down her back and her facial features have a geeky, almost horsy look, but she's still beautiful and innocent.

"Hey, Mr. Metcalf," Alvin greets me.

"Hey, Alvin," I tell him. "How are you doing?"

McKenna hugs both children and then pushes them away. "You two go finish packing up your rooms while I talk to Mr. Metcalf."

The two children run away. McKenna doesn't open the conversation. She turns her back on me, picks up a box off the living room floor, and carries it to the open-plan dining room table where she starts putting books into the box.

She didn't invite me in, but she didn't slam the door in my face, either. I follow her inside. "Are you moving?" I ask. "Why? Is this because of your diagnosis?"

"You shouldn't be here, Mr. Metcalf," she replies over her shoulder. "You should go back to work. I'm sure you have better things to do than to track me down asking a lot of personal questions."

"Will you please stop calling me that?! You do actually still work for me, McKenna, which means that you being here in the middle of a workday is actually relevant to my business—unless you're quitting in which case you have no reason not to call me by my first name. What is going on with you? Why are you moving out of your apartment?"

She spins around fast. "Will you please just leave me alone?! I have enough to deal with as it is."

She storms past me, pulls more stuff off the shelves, and carries everything to the table. I have to rush to keep up with her.

"At least tell me if you're even still working for me anymore," I tell her. "Just answer me that much. You might have had the decency to tell me to my face that you were quitting."

She gasps in exasperation, but her voice chokes just a little bit when she does it. Is she holding back sobs?

"I can't work for you anymore." Now I hear her voice really trembling. "It was nice while it lasted, but I can't. I just want to spend as much time as I can with my children in the time I have left."

"I can understand that. Why didn't you just tell me that a week ago?"

"I couldn't face you." Her features spasm. She won't even look at me. "I feel terrible that I'm leaving you in the lurch."

"You aren't leaving me in the lurch at all. I told you I want to help you if I can. Do you have some family you can move in with or something? Where are you moving to? Your family lives in Michigan, don't they?"

She compresses her lips. She doesn't even pretend to be exasperated anymore. She fights back tears. "My family is all dead, Mr. Metcalf," she stammers. "I don't have anyone."

I frown at her. "Where will you go, then?"

She jolts away from me, grabs another box, and brings that one to the table, too. She stays on the other side of the table so she doesn't come near me.

"I'm moving into a homeless shelter if you really must know. I have a small amount of money saved up and I don't want to waste it on rent. I want to take my children out and have some nice experiences before they have to go into foster care. That's the truth. You wanted to know. There it is. I don't have any relatives or support. Their father isn't in the picture, so I don't really have any other options. I just have to make the best of it and so do they."

I gape at her in sinking horror. "You can't be serious."

She spins around and waves my reaction away. "That's just the way it is. It isn't ideal, I know, but I don't have any other relatives, so that's the way it has to be."

I pace over to her. I have to stop myself from grabbing her and shaking her. "You do have support, McKenna. I told you I wanted to help you. You don't have to do this alone. I can help you."

She snorts and walks away from me. "Please. I'm sure you have better things to do than to mess around with me."

"I'm not messing around, McKenna!" I hear my voice rising and fight it under control. "I....I have a place you can stay. You don't have to go into a shelter—and it won't cost you anything. I have another house on my estate. It's by a lake. You can stay there."

She narrows her eyes and glares at me. "Your estate? Seriously? Is this your way of trying to start something with me—with a woman who's terminally ill?"

"Will you stop that?! You can stay there alone for all I care. I won't ever visit you unless you want me to. Come on, McKenna. Just let me do something to help you. It's the least I can do in exchange for all the years of good work you've done for me."

She shrugs that off. "I didn't do it out of the kindness of my heart. I did it for a paycheck."

"It was still valuable to me. Come on. I can set your children up so they don't have to go into foster care. You can't possibly convince me that you want that for them. Let me help you. Please. I can't let this happen to you—or them. What do you think—that I can stand by and watch your family go down the drain without doing something to stop it? Come on. Please. I'm begging you."

She looks down at the box in front of her and compresses her lips. She keeps her head turned so I can't see her reaction.

Don't ask me what I'll do if she turns me down. I might just have to watch from afar and step in once she dies. No way in hell will I let her children go into foster care because of this. I would even go so far as to take them into my own home and raise them as my own.

I don't tell her that. She won't have anything to say about it after she's gone. They'll need me then and I'll damn well be there when it happens.

I just hope she's sensible enough to realize she doesn't have to wait that long.

She looks up, stares toward the window, and tears streak down her cheeks. I walk over to her, but I stop myself from putting my arms around her. I want to, but we're really just acquaintances. I can't even call her my friend.

I settle for resting my hand on her shoulder. "Just let me take you somewhere nice. You can live there for as long as you want—no obligations. I just want you to be comfortable and not have to worry about anything. Come on. Don't do this to your children. They don't deserve this."

She compresses her lips, looks down, and nods. She's crying too hard to answer. I don't need any other answer. This is terrible—for her a lot more than for me.

Her kids come into the room just then. I'm standing in front of their mother so they don't see her crying.

"Mom, have you seen my swimming goggles?" Evie asks.

I turn around and position myself so they still can't see McKenna. "We've had a change of plans, kids. You aren't going to a shelter after all."

"We aren't?" Alvin and his sister exchange glances. "Where are we going?"

"I know of a house on Long Island where you and your mom are going to stay. You kids help your mom finish packing. I have to go back to work. I'll come around about five o'clock, pick you up, and take you to your new place. Okay? I'll see you later."

"I've never been to Long Island before," Alvin remarks.

"Well, you're about to find out what it's like. Help your mom get this place packed up and I'll see you this afternoon."

I walk out of the building, get back into my car, and return to the office. I spend the next half an hour making phone calls that have nothing to do with my business.

First, I hire a moving company to take all of McKenna's and her children's belongings to my estate on Long Island. I make a few more phone calls to arrange everything they'll need. At least she realizes she doesn't have to push everyone away because of her diagnosis.

Chapter 3:
McKenna

I glance up and immediately look away when Jackson steps into my apartment. It's empty except for the furniture. I can only mumble, "Thank you." Those words don't begin to cover how grateful I am for his help.

The moving company has been coming and going all afternoon to take my stuff to his lake house. I don't know what to expect once we get there.

The kids come into the living room before I have a chance to say anything else. "Are we really going to Long Island now?" Alvin asks.

"Yes, we are," Jackson tells him. "Grab your suitcases and let's get motoring."

The kids won't stop talking. They act like we're going on a road trip or something. I don't know how much they've fully accepted the fact that I have a terminal illness. They're still too thrilled that they don't have to go to school anymore.

They wheel their suitcases out of their bedrooms. Jackson leads the way to the elevator. I come last. I don't know how to deal with him now. He isn't my boss anymore. He isn't even really a friend. He's just a concerned citizen.

The kids talk all the way down to the street. Jackson's black Range Rover sits parked at the curb. Alvin goes into convulsions when he sees the car.

Jackson talks about cars while he opens the back and puts all three of our suitcases inside. I catch him watching me, but I can't hold eye contact with him.

Some part of me thinks I should be handling this better. I should be the one making plans for my children so they don't have to go into foster care after I'm gone. I shouldn't have to rely on a man who is essentially a total stranger.

Jackson opens the front passenger door for me to get in. The kids climb into the back seat. I cringe when I see Jackson acting so chivalrously toward me. He does it to everyone, but it just makes me feel weak, poor, and helpless.

He starts the engine and drives across town toward Long Island. He talks back and forth to the kids the whole time. He tells them all about his mining operations all over the world and what substance or mineral each mine produces.

The kids get super excited by everything he tells them—and then they see the surrounding countryside as we get closer to his estate.

They can hardly believe it when he turns off into the driveway. He has to drive a long way through the grounds before they see his giant mansion.

"Holy mackerel!" Alvin breathes. "You actually live there?!"

"I don't live in all of it, of course. I use some parts of it more than others."

I try not to make a big deal about the mansion, either. I've seen what it looks like inside. He holds company events here. The guy has more money than God Himself.

Jackson drives around the mansion and continues down a long road to the lake in the distance. I haven't been to this part of his estate.

I have to stop myself from gasping and exclaiming in amazement when I see the lake house. The kids don't even try to hide their shock.

"Oh, my God!" Evie gushes. "It's huge!"

"The movers put all your stuff inside already," Jackson tells them. "I guess you guys can arm-wrestle for which bedroom you want."

"This is incredible!" Alvin shoots his arm out. "Look! This place even has its own boathouse! Could we go sailing—or windsurfing—or kayaking?"

"Sure," Jackson replies. "I can take you on the weekends."

"Are those stables?" Evie asks from the opposite window. "Ooo, look at the horses running around!"

"Do you like horses?" Jackson asks. "You could go riding. You just go over there and talk to Marcus. He's the head groom. He can set you up."

"No way!" she gasps. "This is incredible!"

Jackson parks in front of the lake house. A big deck opens onto the lake side of the house. Giant folding doors stand open to let us walk from the deck into the huge living room with a modern, open kitchen across the back.

Stairs rise from there to a wooden railing leading to the upstairs bedrooms. The master bedroom occupies a spot off the side of the living room with another small private deck facing the lake.

The kids gasp and exclaim some more when they see the big deer-antler chandelier hanging over the living room, the log walls with all the decorations, and a high-tech electronic entertainment center across from the living room couches.

The kids spread out to explore the house. They keep going out onto the deck to look at the lake and shield their eyes from the sun.

I try not to get too goggle-eyed over all of this. I've seen Jackson's lifestyle from the fringes. I've never experienced it before—not like this.

The lake house is bigger, fancier, and more palatial than any other house, residence, or apartment I've ever seen—except for his mansion, of course. I don't want to believe that my children and I are actually going to live here—for as long as I have left to live.

The kids go back out to the deck. Alvin splits off to the right to go explore around the lake. Evie heads left toward the stables.

I turn around to thank him again—and discover him watching me. His eyes pinch with concern, but he doesn't say anything about that.

I don't want him feeling that way about me. I don't want him to treat me like I'm helpless and can't support my family on my own—which I can't.

I'm just about to open my mouth to say that this is all too much and he shouldn't be going to such lengths. The kids come back just then and start bombarding him with comments about everything they're seeing outside.

I pull Alvin closer to me. "You kids thank Mr. Metcalf for this," I tell them. "He's letting us live here."

"Thanks, Mr. Metcalf," Alvin exclaims. "This place is awesome."

"You can call me Jackson," Jackson tells them—and looks up at me. "You can all call me that. You don't work for me anymore."

"Thanks, Jackson," Evie breathes. "Could I really ride the horses sometime?"

"You bet." He turns away. "I have an idea. I'll bring some groceries over for dinner tonight. Then I'll take you out tomorrow and we can do all the stuff you want to. I know your mom was planning to take you out, so we can start with all the stuff you want to do on the estate. I'll be back in a little while. Settle in and make yourselves at home."

He walks out jangling his car keys in his hand, gets in his car, and drives away.

The kids keep going around the house looking at absolutely everything. They find a pantry stacked with all kinds of food, a fridge full of snacks, staples, and drinks, and even ice cream in the fridge.

Alvin wants to mess around with the entertainment system, but I tell him to leave it alone. Then the two kids go back outside. Their happy, excited voices drift from down by the lake.

I lower myself onto the couch. I feel tired, but the overwhelming sense of relief overpowers everything else. I don't have to worry about taking care of my family anymore.

I don't know how to deal with Jackson. I feel guilty for accepting his generosity, but he would be offended if I didn't. I really do need this. He's too kind and caring not to notice that.

This house is magnificent and the setting is relaxing, luxurious, and comforting. I rest my head on the couch cushions and gaze out at the lake. I don't have to worry about anything anymore—except the fact that I won't be able to enjoy this for long.

Chapter 4: Jackson

I park my car next to the lake house, pop the back, and take out a big box of groceries. I've already stocked the lake house with all the food McKenna and her children will need, but I don't want to burn through her supplies by making them dinner.

I carry the box and two others into the kitchen. The doors stand open to the deck, but I don't hear anyone around. McKenna and the kids aren't here.

I'm just unpacking the third box when I spot the three of them on the opposite side of the lake. She sits on the shore while Alvin skips stones on the surface. Evie squats next to the water poking something with a stick.

That's good. I'm glad they can settle in, relax, and enjoy themselves here. All three of them need that.

I start making dinner in the kitchen. I take out pots and pans, cut up vegetables, and stick a loaf of garlic bread in the oven. Then I put the extra staples in the pantry. I see some of the junk food snacks already missing. Good. The kids must be eating it.

I have my back turned to the deck when I hear a child's shout echoing across the water. I take a break from cooking to go over there and check to see where they are.

They're standing in front of the boathouse pointing through the windows. Then Alvin waves his arms toward the water.

I chuckle to myself and go back to the kitchen. This place is going to be good for all of them. I bet her kids never got to do anything like this while they were living in Manhattan.

They don't come back for another hour. I'm just setting the table as the sun goes down when the three of them climb onto the deck.

The kids gape at me in wide-eyed shock when they see me in the kitchen. "Um...what are you doing?" Evie asks.

"You can see what I'm doing," I tell them. "I'm making dinner. I'm sure you've seen your mom doing it hundreds of times."

"Yeah...but....she's our mom," Alvin tells me. "You're...."

"I'm what?" I ask. "I can cook the same as she can."

"But you're a guy," Evie points out.

"So?" I ask. "I don't see an invisible force field that blocks men from cooking in the kitchen." I point at Alvin. "Remember this, kid. Women respect a man who knows his way around the kitchen."

McKenna laughs in the background and sits down on the couch in the living room. "I can't wait to hear this."

"What are you making?" Evie asks.

"It's an ancient secret recipe from the mountains of my home country," I tell her. "I can't tell you what's in it or I might have to kill you to keep it a secret."

"What country is that?" Alvin asks. "You don't talk with an accent or anything."

"Unfortunately, that's a government secret, too. I'm not allowed to tell anyone."

McKenna laughs again. Evie notices, turns around to look at her mom, and then narrows her eyes at me. "I don't believe you. I think you made that up."

"You can't prove that. I bet none of you knows where I'm really from."

"My mom said you were from Oregon originally," Evie counters.

I can't help but laugh. "Dang."

"So what are you making?" Alvin insists.

"It's something you've probably never heard of. We call it, 'spaghetti' in my country."

Both kids laugh. "This is your country, Jackson," Alvin tells me.

I try to shrug that off. "So what's on the schedule for tomorrow besides horseback riding, sailing, windsurfing, and kayaking? I hope you both have swimsuits."

"We do," Alvin replies.

"Will we have time for anything else?" Evie asks. "How long will that take?"

"We can always do some of it the next day if we need to."

"Don't we have to go back to school?" Alvin asks. "Mom said she doesn't know...."

He trails off. He doesn't say the words out loud.

"Let's just see how it goes for now," I tell him. "I suppose it depends on how your mom feels and how she wants to spend her time with you. One or both of you might decide you want to go back to school just so you can live your normal lives the way you used to. It just depends. There's no rulebook for stuff like this."

"Don't *you* have to work tomorrow?" McKenna calls from the living room. "And the day after that?"

I shoot her a look across the room. "You aren't in charge of my schedule anymore. Besides, some things are more important than work."

She looks away from me.

"Do you know how to windsurf, Jackson?" Alvin asks me.

"I know how, but I'm too big and heavy to do it well. I like sailing better."

"Why are you so big?" Evie asks.

I laugh at her. "That's my giant blood coming through. Didn't your mom tell you that part of the story? My dad went on a journey through the mountains of Oregon, lived with a tribe of giants for a while, and that's how I was born."

"You're making that up!" Alvin counters.

I grin at him. "You'll probably think I'm making it up if I tell you I was once your size—and I was even smaller when I was younger. You might get to be as big as me and then you'll have little girls asking why you're so big."

"You do not have giant blood," Evie sneers. "That's impossible."

"Have you ever been to Oregon?"

"No, but I know there aren't any giants living there."

"How would you know if you've never been there? You probably think there aren't leprechauns living in Central Park, either."

"No, there aren't!" Alvin insists. "Stop making up stories."

"There are. I've seen them with my own eyes. They splash around in the fountains on hot days and drop their ice cream cones all over the sidewalk."

"Those are just little kids!" Evie counters. "They aren't leprechauns!"

I pretend to frown. "Really? Oh. My mistake, then."

They both laugh. I finish setting the table and tell the kids to go wash their hands for dinner. I catch McKenna watching me from the living room. She's actually smiling at me.

I look away and concentrate on putting dinner on the table. She and the kids sit down and I bow my head to say grace. I look up and discover all three of them staring at me.

"What?" I ask.

"We never do anything like that at home," Alvin tells me.

"Oh. Sorry." I grab the serving spoons for the salad. "You can go back to not doing it as soon as I leave."

"Are you too big and heavy to ride horses, too, Jackson?" Evie asks me.

"No, I like riding horses. That's why I bought a place with stables—so I could ride in all the free time I don't have from my work."

"So when do you ride?" Alvin asks.

"Hardly ever—but I do have some schools and other children's educational programs that come out and ride on a regular basis. There's a lady down the road here who runs a program taking abused and neglected kids horseback riding. It helps them recover from their experiences. They come here—and I have a few programs for kids with intellectual disabilities to ride. The horses don't lack for people to ride them. That's for certain."

"That sounds nice," Evie remarks.

"They certainly enjoy it." I turn to McKenna. "What would you like to do while you're here? What's on your bucket list?"

She pushes her food around on her plate. "I don't have one."

"Well, now you can start making one. Do you want to climb Mount Kilimanjaro?"

She snorts. "I don't think I have the energy for that."

"What's Mount Kilimanjaro?" Alvin asks. "Did you make up that, too?"

"No, it's a real place. You can look it up on the internet. It's in Africa—on the western side in Kenya."

His eyes widen. "Really? I want to do that."

"Start with conquering Long Island first." I turn back to McKenna. "Are you sure there's nothing you want to do?"

"I'll just enjoy seeing you all do it," she replies.

I let the matter drop. The kids start holding forth about all the stuff on *their* bucket lists. They have a lot they want to do. McKenna keeps quiet for most of the meal unless someone asks her a specific question.

I catch her watching me talk to her kids. I hope she doesn't think I'm invading their privacy by having dinner with them.

I want to reassure her that I won't do it again. I just want to welcome them and make them feel at home this first night—and I have a few other reasons up my sleeve.

I want her kids to get to know me. I want them to get familiar with me so they won't be too shocked when I step in after she dies. I don't want them to think of me as a stranger. I want them to feel like someone they know is taking care of them.

I get the kids to help me clean up the kitchen and dining table after we eat. McKenna sits quietly off to one side watching and listening.

I find it easy to talk to her kids, make them laugh, and get them interested in all kinds of stuff. I don't worry about establishing a connection with them.

She finally comes over to the kitchen counter and tells them it's time for them to get ready for bed. She takes them upstairs to their bedrooms while I finish putting the dishes and pans away.

I catch snatches of their conversation.

"Are you and Jackson going to get married?" Alvin asks.

She laughs nervously. "No, sweetheart. He just wants to do something nice for us."

"He's a nice person," Evie remarks. "He's really easy to talk to."

I start the dishwasher so I don't overhear anything else. She comes downstairs in a little while just as I'm drying my hands on a towel.

"I'll get out of your hair," I tell her. "Think about what I said about what you want to do with your time. We can make it happen as long as it isn't something like going to the moon or curing world hunger."

She laughs. "I'll try to keep it realistic."

I head for the door. "You have my number if you need anything. I'm right over there on the other side of the hill."

I walk out, get in my car, and drive back to my place. I would like to stay up and get some work done, but I have to get some sleep tonight so I'll be ready for tomorrow. I have a big day in front of me.

Chapter 5: McKenna

Jackson knocks on the lake house door and sticks his head in. "Helloooo! Is anyone home?"

"No," I tell him from the kitchen.

The kids come barreling in just then. They bounce around in front of him. They talk extra loudly about what they're going to do today. Each of them wants to do their own activity first.

"I already told Evie we would ride first," Jackson tells Alvin. "Don't worry. The lake won't dry up before we get there."

"Do we have to wear special clothes to go riding?" Evie asks. "Do we have to wear special pants and boots and jackets?"

"That's stupid," Alvin counters. "The horses don't care what you wear."

"You can wear what you have on," Jackson tells her. "They have boots and helmets at the stables. Marcus will fit you out with whatever gear you need." He looks up at me. "Are you ready?"

I nod and follow the three of them outside. The kids jump up and down all around Jackson on our way to the stables.

I hang back. I can't get near him with the kids there and I don't feel comfortable enough to go near him anyway. I don't feel comfortable about any of this.

Evie races away and gets to the corral fence first. Jackson has some beautiful horses and they come over to greet her. She pets them.

The rest of us join her and Jackson gives her some lumps of brown sticky squares to feed them. "What is it?" she asks.

"It's a treat for them, but it's more nutritious and not as bad for their teeth as feeding them sugar, apples, and carrots. Come on. Let's go see Marcus and get you suited up."

The kids talk all the way up to the stables and then laugh when the horses follow us. Jackson talks about each of the horses in detail. He knows all their names.

"Have you ridden all of these horses?" Alvin asks.

Jackson nods. "Yep. I wanted to find out which one was my favorite."

"Which is?" Alvin asks.

Jackson points to a black gelding in the back. "Him. His name is Ulysses. He has spirit. He isn't above charging around and getting wild when you want that in a horse—and I like her. Her name is Ursula. She's the same. Some of these horses like to live the quiet life."

"Ursula!" Evie snorts. "What kind of a name is that?"

"I think it's Greek," Jackson replies.

"Are you sure it isn't an ancient name from the hidden mountains of Oregon?" I tease.

He spins around and stares at me, but a tall, older man comes out of the stables just then and distracts us. Jackson introduces us to Marcus. He smiles at the kids and leads them inside to get them fitted out with all the appropriate riding gear.

"Do you want to ride?" Jackson asks me.

"I think I better not."

He frowns. "Are you that tired? These horses are trained to carry kids with mental disabilities. You won't get bucked off or anything."

"It isn't that. I don't want to make this about me."

He opens his mouth to say something, but the kids interrupt again by coming out of the barn just then. They won't stop talking about all the saddles and bridles Marcus has been showing them in the tack room.

The kids' commotion covers up that I'm not taking part in all of this. Jackson gets a pair of boots and a helmet for himself. Then he and Marcus go out into the pasture and come back with three horses. One of them is Ulysses. The other two are mares—not Ursula.

Marcus and Jackson show the kids how to groom, saddle, and bridle the horses, how to handle them, and how to walk around them so the kids don't startle the animals. Jackson has to constantly remind both kids to move slowly and quietly so the horses stay calm.

The two mares are named Blossom and Cheddar. "What kind of a name is Cheddar for a horse?" Evie demands. "Who would name a horse after a kind of cheese?"

"It's a place in England," Jackson tells her.

"It is not!" she groans.

He stops where he is, pulls his phone out of his pocket, and navigates to something on his maps app. He shows her the screen. "Read 'em and weep, young Padawan."

She makes a face. "I'm not a Padawan."

"Maybe you should be. Climb up on that block and mount up."

She leads Cheddar to the mounting block, climbs the steps, and climbs into the saddle. Cheddar stands there in placid acceptance of everything. She and Blossom act like a nuclear explosion wouldn't startle them.

Ulysses is a completely different story. Jackson mounts from the ground. Ulysses tosses his head and paces in a circle until Jackson steers the horse over to the two children. "Let's go," Jackson orders.

Both kids kick their horses way too hard, but the horses pretend not to notice. They've seen it all before.

Jackson has to control Ulysses. Blossom and Cheddar plod after him on their way out to the fields. I lean on the corral fence and watch them go. I'm glad Alvin and Evie can enjoy these days and have some nice memories to take with them after I'm gone.

I'm grateful to Jackson for giving them this—and I'm glad they're connecting with him. I've always known he was a nice person. It just makes me uncomfortable that he's the one doing it instead of me.

I don't tell him or my children that I've never ridden a horse and I'm not about to start. I don't trust anything that big that has a mind of its own. I also don't want to get that far off the ground.

I don't mind seeing my children doing it for some reason. I don't think they're in danger. Jackson stays with them and I couldn't ask for two more docile mounts than Blossom and Cheddar. They never even break into a trot.

They ride all over the property and the two kids come back beaming from ear to ear. "You should have come, Mom!" Alvin tells me. "That was awesome!"

"You can come back anytime," Jackson tells him. "You can just tell Marcus and he'll set you up—as long as one of the other groups isn't here. They use most of the horses, so you should probably come when they aren't here."

He helps the kids dismount, unsaddle and unbridle the horses, groom them down, put them back in the corral, and give them treats before we leave. "Do we have time to go sailing before lunch?" he asks.

Alvin jumps up and down pumping his fists. "Yeah! Let's do that!"

Jackson leads the way back to the boathouse. He and Alvin go into a lengthy discussion about which boat they're going to take.

Evie stays on dry land with me while Jackson and Alvin launch the boat. They stay out there for two hours crisscrossing the lake in all directions. I hear Jackson telling Alvin all about the parts of the boat and explaining how to do everything.

Evie and I sit on the grass to wait for the two of them to finish. They stay out for so long that we wind up bringing a bunch of food outside and setting up a picnic lunch on the grass.

"Jackson is really nice," Evie remarks while we wait. "I remember you saying that when you worked for him, but now I see how really nice he is."

"Yes, he is," I agree. "He's one of the nicest people I know—but he can get stern when people don't do what he tells them to do."

Her eyes widen. "Did he ever do that to you?"

"No, no! Nothing like that. I'm talking about if he told one of his employees what to do and they didn't do it. He doesn't like that."

"Well, he's the boss, isn't he?" She falls silent for a minute. "I wouldn't mind if you did marry him."

I make a face to cover up how uncomfortable the subject makes me. "I don't have time to marry anyone, sweetheart. Besides, Jackson and I don't have a relationship like that."

"But you could. You could have a relationship like that." She stares out at the water. "I can't imagine you having one with someone better than him."

"I'm not getting into a relationship with anyone. That wouldn't be fair considering I'm not going to be around to be there for them."

She doesn't answer. We sit in silence until Jackson and Alvin put the boat away and join us.

"Can we windsurf after this?" Alvin asks while we eat.

"We could, but we should probably do something that Evie and your mom want to do," Jackson replies.

"I want to windsurf," Evie interjects.

Jackson's eyes widen. "You do? Okay." He turns to me. "Do you want to windsurf?"

I laugh. "No, thank you. I'll stay here and make fun of all of you when you fall in the water."

"We won't fall in," Alvin tells me.

"Yes, you will," Jackson replies. "Everyone falls in when they first start."

"Did you fall in?" Evie asks.

"Sure. I fell in lots of times. That's just part of learning."

"I don't believe you," Alvin counters.

"I'll probably fall in today. I'm out of practice. Then you can all laugh at me."

The kids joke about that while we finish lunch. Then Jackson sends them up to the lake house to change into their swimsuits.

He drives up to his house and comes back in a pair of board shorts and a T-shirt. I find myself eyeing him on the side. This is the most casual I've seen him ever. He never wears anything but a suit to work every day.

I've seen him wearing business casual at certain less formal events, but never like this.

He pulls three windsurfing boards out of the boathouse. One is adult sized and the other two are obviously made for kids. He sets the boards parallel to each other at the water's edge while he explains to the kids what they have to do.

He gets them to stand on their boards and shows them how to pull on ropes to lift their sails. Then he explains how to turn their sails into the wind to steer and change direction.

He puts his arms around Alvin and holds onto the guide bar just long enough for the wind to pull the board out onto the water's surface. Alvin stays upright for thirty seconds before he loses control and falls.

Evie laughs at him. "No big deal!" Jackson calls. "Just climb up onto the board and do it again. You'll get the hang of it."

He goes over to Evie, does the same thing, and she falls, too. Both kids get soaked in a matter of minutes.

Jackson goes over to his own board and pulls off his T-shirt. This is the first time I've ever seen him with his shirt off. He's built like a tank—and that's nothing compared to what he looks like when he uses his muscles to steer his board.

He pushes it into the water, steps onto it, and leans back to hold the sail in the right position. He stays on much longer, skims out across the water, and makes it all the way to the other side of the lake.

He gets into trouble when he moves the sail to stall the board and tries to switch around to its other side to sail back over to our side of the lake. He loses control and biffs.

Both kids laugh at him, but they aren't having any better success. They both stay on board for a few seconds each time before they fall off.

He rides back over to each of them, encourages them, and helps lift them onto their boards to make it easy for them. He gets water all over his face and it soaks his hair. I never let myself see before how handsome he is.

His hair falls in his eyes and he shakes his head sideways to flick it out of his eyes. His shoulders stick out of the water and his arms swell when he pulls himself back onto his board.

I don't let myself think of him that way—but I'm starting to think of him that way. He isn't my boss anymore.

No one has ever done anything for me that comes close to this. He's giving my children their dream memories—memories that will last them a lifetime. I can never repay him for this—and that's nothing compared to what he's doing for me.

I can't imagine any better way to end my life than to see my children happy, carefree, and enjoying themselves doing exactly what they want to do. They are obviously loving the experience. They laugh and scream when they fall into the water.

I hear them talking to Jackson when he goes over to help them. He treads water near them, reassures them, and he doesn't hesitate to touch them when he puts them back on their boards.

Evie is too tired to windsurf after her third fall. He puts her on the board and she sits there talking to him while she catches her breath and he bobs in the water nearby.

The connection between them is palpable. He acts like this is all natural for him—like he belongs in their lives.

I can't resent him for getting close to them when he said he would back off and leave us alone. He's giving them so much happiness. I could never rob them of that.

Chapter 6: McKenna

Jackson eventually has to tow the two kids back to shore while they sit on their windsurfing boards. They're too exhausted to surf anymore.

He uses his powerful arms to stroke through the water while he pulls them back to the boathouse and parks them on the beach. He does it with Evie first, goes back for Alvin, and then surfs his own board the normal way.

"You make it look so easy, Jackson," Evie mumbles.

"I've had a lot more practice than you have, sweetie. It's like anything else. You have to practice and learn before you get good enough to really do it right."

He takes their towels, dries them off, and sends them up to the lake house to change while he puts their boards away. He sits down next to me while he waits.

I only get a sense of his size and strength when he sits down next to me with his shirt off. Water droplets sparkle on his skin and split the sunshine into a million glistening diamonds.

Everything about him breathes with pure male energy and power. I never noticed it before in all the years I worked for him. He just seemed like another guy in a suit.

I never even really let myself understand and believe that he had a male body underneath that suit. He sure is attractive, but he's totally out of reach, especially to me.

For one thing, he's a billionaire. He commands empires and moves in the highest circles of influence and power. Someone like that isn't even in the same league with someone like me.

It's interesting that he's never dated anyone or been in a relationship for as long as I've known him. I wonder why not. He never talks about it. He never shows interest in anyone.

He isn't the only member of The Billionaires' Club who lives that way, but he could have any woman he wants. He doesn't have to live alone. Maybe he wants that.

I don't know why I'm even thinking about that because I'm not interested in him. I'm not interested in anything except living the rest of my life.

He glances over at me and our eyes meet for one second before Evie comes out onto the deck behind us. "Mom! I can't find my jeans with the flower on them."

"Check your drawers," I tell her.

"I already did. I checked my whole room."

I groan and Jackson laughs. "Duty calls," he teases.

I start to stand up when another wave of dizziness rushes to my head. I feel myself starting to fall. Jackson leaps up and grabs me. "McKenna!" His voice shakes.

He lowers me back down onto the grass, lays me on my back, and stares down into my face from above. Is Evie seeing me like this? Is she seeing him bending over me like we're a couple?

"Talk to me!" he breathes. "Stay with me. I'm calling an ambulance."

"No...." I choke and struggle to sit up. "I'm okay."

"You should lie down. You could pass out again."

"I didn't pass out. I'm okay."

I sit up and push his hands and arms away from me. I don't want to see him hovering over me. I do still feel weak and shaky. I don't trust myself to stand up, but Evie isn't on the deck anymore. She must have gone inside.

Jackson doesn't back off, but he doesn't touch me again, either. He just squats in front of me staring into my eyes. "You really should go to the hospital."

"I don't want to spend the whole time in the hospital." I drag my vision into focus. "I'll be all right. Just give me a minute."

He sits down on the grass in front of me. He's completely oblivious to how hot he is. He doesn't see anything out of the ordinary about the way he's acting toward me. Making a move on me is the absolute last thing on his mind.

Him sitting so near me with his shirt off makes me a lot more uncomfortable than if he had his clothes on. I can't even tell him to put his shirt on. That would give too much away.

He doesn't say anything or suggest again that I go to the hospital. The dizziness fades and Alvin and Evie come out of the house together in a little while.

I spend a few minutes sitting down to gather up all the lunch stuff. I stand up more slowly this time and get the kids to help me carry everything back to the house.

Jackson takes that opportunity to put his shirt on, tells us all that he's going up to his house to change, and that he'll see us later.

The kids and I take it easy around the house for the rest of the day. All this excitement and activity makes them subdued. That gives me the perfect opportunity to lounge on the couch and rest. How did I get so weak all of a sudden?

Whatever is wrong with me seems to be escalating a lot more quickly, now that I know what it is. I never noticed anything wrong with me before—or maybe I just explained it away by saying I was stressed and tired from raising two kids on my own.

I make dinner by myself. Jackson doesn't come this time.

"Why isn't Jackson coming for dinner tonight?" Evie asks.

"I don't know, sweetie. Maybe he had something come up with work. He's very busy. Besides, the three of us need to spend time together. Jackson doesn't want to intrude on that."

"He should come," Alvin insists. "I want him to. I like having him here."

"Me, too," Evie adds. "Having him here is like having a real family."

I don't know what to say. I push my food around on my plate.

"Plus he knows everything about boats," Alvin goes on. "He's fun to talk to—about everything."

"I know!" Evie agrees and they both start talking about all the stuff they did with Jackson today.

I don't know what to tell them. Having Jackson around certainly livens things up, but I'm not ready to share my children with anyone, not even him.

The kids spend the rest of the evening in their rooms doing their own thing. I'm sitting on the couch reading a book at seven o'clock when Jackson comes back. He couldn't make it more obvious that he was waiting until after dinner to come over.

He comes in wearing immaculate business casual clothes. He dresses impeccably even when he keeps it casual. He steps through the open deck doors carrying a black leather zipper folio. I've seen that before.

I sit up and put my book away to greet him. "Hey. You missed dinner."

"I was wondering if you have a minute to talk." He looks around. "Talk uninterrupted, I mean."

"The kids are winding down upstairs. I don't think they'll be interested in anything you want to talk about." I frown at him and then eye his case. "What's on your mind?"

He sits down on the couch and unzips his case on the coffee table in front of me. "I want to talk to you about the kids and their future." He pulls out a glossy pamphlet. It reads, *Heritage Academy.* "This is all the information for a residential boarding school in Upper Manhattan. I'll pay for the kids to go there after you're gone. They can come back here and spend vacations and holidays with me. I don't want you to think I'm trying to horn in on the time you have left with them. I just want to build a bond with them so they aren't totally alone after they don't have you anymore. I want us to be bonded by our connection to you. We can help each other get over your loss and keep your memory alive together. I hope you don't think I'm overstepping here, but I just can't stand to see them go to strangers or into the foster system."

I stare at the pamphlet in front of me. I know all about Heritage Academy. I would never be able to send my children there.

I can't think of any better future they could have than what he's describing. They'll get a much better education there than they would at their current school—and they'll have Jackson to come home to when they aren't at school.

I can't even react to the news. Why am I even surprised that he would go to such lengths?

He's set up endowments, trust funds, and college funds with his money before. Of course he would want to do something like this—and he's already building that bond with my children. They know him. They like him. They trust him. What's not to like?

He waits for me to say something. I can't even look at him. I might by some miracle have been able to save enough money to send them to Heritage Academy after I die.

I would never be able to find someone to take care of them, watch over them, and look out for them the way he will. No amount of money could buy that.

I know he respects me and even cares for me. He's been showing me that every day for years. My children would know that after I die and they go to live with him.

They would share that with him. They would know that he remembered me the way they do and that he's doing all of this because of his connection to me.

He waits for me to react, and when I don't, he jumps back into his case and turns to a few other plain white sheets of paper. "I've set up trust funds for each of them so they'll always be taken care of and you don't have to worry about what's going to happen to them."

I put the pamphlet down on the table and look away. "I don't know what to say, Jackson." My voice trembles. "I could never thank you enough for this."

"I don't want thanks." Now he's the one who turns away. "I never thought I would ever get to do any of this with children of my own. I'm always too busy with work. Now I'm finding it by doing it with you and your family. I'm getting as much out of this as you are—maybe even more."

I turn around and realize that I'm looking into his eyes at close range. "Thank you," I murmur. "Thank you for all of this. You have no idea how much this means to me."

"You have no idea how much you mean to me. I could never let anything bad happen to you or your children. Just accept this. It's the least I can do."

I can only nod. This is beyond anything I thought possible. It lifts the last burden from my shoulders. I can finally just be okay with what's about to happen because my children will be taken care of no matter what.

Chapter 7: McKenna

I sit down on the couch in front of my children and face them.

"What's going on, Mom?" Alvin asks. "Did something happen?"

"Of course it did," Evie tells her brother. "Something already did happen. She's going to die. What could be worse than that?"

"Nothing happened," I tell them. "I just...I need to talk to you both....honestly. We need to be honest with ourselves and talk straight. I love you both too much to keep anything from you—not anything really important."

They exchange glances. They don't like where this is going and neither do I.

"You both know that I've never had a lot of money," I begin. "I worked hard to keep a roof over your heads and to give you everything you needed. I never had much extra—which means I don't have a lot of money to pay for the things you might need after I'm gone. You both understand that, don't you?"

"Yeah?" Alvin asks. "We never needed money before."

"We might need it now." I pull out the pamphlet from Heritage Academy. "This is a residential boarding school in uptown Manhattan. The students live there during the school year and go home to their families for vacations and holiday weekends. Jackson is offering to send you both there after I'm gone. Then you would come back here and treat his house as your home when you aren't at school. He wants to be there as your guardian to help you, guide you, and give you a home when I'm not here to give it to you anymore."

The two kids exchange glances again. They don't react to the news.

"He cares about me and he cares about you too much to let you go into the foster system or for any strangers to take care of you," I choke. "He wants to be there for you and for you to know that the person responsible for you knew and respected me and that he's doing this is a way to honor me. He wants to share that with you. See? He's set up trust funds for you to support you no matter what happens so you'll always be taken care of."

The two kids stare at me and then look down at the pamphlet. They don't say anything at first.

"So what do you think about all of that?" I ask.

"I guess so," Alvin mumbles.

"You guess so what?" I ask. "What do you think about Jackson stepping in and being your guardian after I'm gone?"

"I guess it's better than going to strangers," Evie murmurs. "Jackson's really nice."

"I guess it does help that he knows what our family was like before....I mean..." Alvin trails off. "I guess he's better than nothing, isn't he—but he isn't you. I don't want Jackson. I want you."

"I know, sweetheart." I put my arms around him and blink back tears. "I want you, too. I don't want anyone else taking care of you, not even him. I want you both all to myself."

I gather both my children in my arms. We share a three-way hug for a minute. I can't help but shed a few tears when I sit back and face them.

"I just want you both to know where this is going. I want you both to know that you're covered and that you'll be taken care of afterward. You won't go anywhere. You'll stay here with him until it's time for you to go to school. Okay?"

They both nod, but the news devastates both of them. I don't blame them. I feel the same way even though I'm over-the-top grateful to Jackson for doing this.

That's what makes him the perfect solution to all of this. He would understand that they don't want him.

He wouldn't resent them for feeling that way or for any other feelings they would have about his presence. He cares enough to let them feel whatever they need to feel.

I wipe my face and try to act a little more cheerful about this. I don't want my children to spend my last days depressed and living under a cloud. I start to stand up.

"Mom?" Alvin asks.

"Yeah, sweetie?" I sit down in front of him and take his hand. "What's up?"

"I....I want to go back to school. Jackson said we might want to live normal lives. I mean...." His eyes swivel toward the lake. "This place is so nice and everything....but I just want to go to school. I want to see my friends. Hanging out here....it's like.....it's like we're all waiting for something bad to happen."

I gulp at those words. This is the death house. It's basically a much nicer version of a hospice. Who in their right mind would want to live in that?

"Okay, sweetie," I rasp. "We can arrange that."

"I want to go to school, too, Mom," Evie murmurs under her breath. "I just want things to go back to the way they were before even if we can't live in our old apartment."

"Okay, baby." I squeeze both their hands and stroke their cheeks. "Today is Sunday, so why don't you both go upstairs and start getting your stuff ready so you can go back to school tomorrow morning? I'll call the office and explain everything to them."

The two kids go upstairs in subdued silence. They don't run around laughing and admiring the lake house the way they did when we moved in here. Of course not.

The house can't change the fundamental fact of why we need to live here at all. The house itself offers the most painful reminder of exactly what we're all facing. None of us can ignore it anymore.

I go out onto the deck and take a few minutes to bury my face in my hands and cry. I would give absolutely anything to spare my children from this. They shouldn't have to go through this. It isn't fair to them.

I can't even protect them from this—or from anything else. I have nothing to take care of my own children—nothing but my love for them. That's all I have left to give them.

I finally rub my face across my shoulder, pull out my phone, and call Jackson. We both still have each other's numbers from when I worked for him.

"Hello?" he answers.

"Jackson...it's me." Like he doesn't already know that.

"How's it going?" he asks. "Did you tell the kids about my idea?"

"Yeah, I told them. That's not what I'm calling about. They....they want to go back to school.....and I don't have a car to drive them. I sold it when I got my diagnosis—so I would have the money for other things."

"Okay. I'll send a car over tomorrow morning to drive them. You can go with them and then the car will bring you back here for the day. Then the car will take you to pick them up and you can bring them home. Will that work?"

I clamp my eyes shut holding back another surge of heartbreaking anguish. Of course he would do something like this. It never occurs to him not to do anything as long as we need it.

"Yeah," I croak. "That would be great."

"Give me the address of their school so I can tell the driver."

I give it to him. I hear his pen scribbling on paper on the other end of the phone. "Okay. I got it. The trip into town takes about twenty minutes, but it can take longer if the traffic is bad. I'll tell the driver to pick you up at about eight-fifteen. That should give you enough time to get there, say goodbye for the day, and give the kids some extra time to talk to their friends and get to their classes. Okay?"

"Yeah," I choke. "Thank you, Jackson."

"No problem," he murmurs back. "I want you to call me if you need anything—and I mean anything. Understand? I want to do this. I don't want you to think you're doing me a favor by sparing me the trouble and expense."

"Okay," I rasp. "Thank you."

"You can stop saying that. Now hang up and go get ready for tomorrow."

I hang up and break down crying again. I should have known he wouldn't let anything happen to us. He was the one who suggested that the kids might want to go back to school. He's in this for real. He really wants this.

I go back inside and start getting everything ready for tomorrow. I pack the kids' lunches and put their lunchboxes in the fridge overnight.

Eight-fifteen is a lot earlier than they had to leave for school when we lived right down the block. We'll need to be ready to leave in time.

The kids act a lot more normal, now that they know they're going back to school. They talk at their usual volume and even get into a few squabbling matches that I have to intervene and stop.

Maybe going back to school is the right thing for them after all. Jackson is a lot smarter about all of this than I am.

I send the kids to bed early that night. The words, "It's a school night," sound strange coming from me even though it's been less than two weeks since the kids stopped going.

They wake up chipper and ready to rock first thing Monday morning. I make sure they have all their stuff and lunchboxes packed in their backpacks. They won't be able to come home during lunch and I won't be able to stop by and drop off anything they might have forgotten.

A black sedan pulls up to the lake house at ten after eight. We load up and start the drive from Long Island to Manhattan.

Jackson hit the nail on the head about the traffic. We get delayed more than once and pull into the school at exactly quarter to nine—which is perfect. I get out to hug the kids, tell them I love them, and to assure them that I'll be here to pick them up at the usual time.

They don't need to go to the afterschool program, but they both say they want to do that, too. I won't be back until six. That gives me the whole day to myself. I don't even know what I'll do with myself.

I get back in the car. The drive out to the lake house gives me plenty of time to think. This is the most time I've spent by myself since Evie was born.

I get lost in my own thoughts until the car pulls into the driveway at Jackson's estate. I get out by the lake and find Jackson's Range Rover parked there. He's just carrying another huge box of groceries into the house.

"Hello," he greets me when he comes out. "Is everyone ready for the day?"

"Yeah." I can't help smiling at him. "Thank you. This is exactly what they needed."

"I'm not surprised." He squints at me. "What about you? Do you have everything you need?"

"Do you mean apart from something to occupy myself today? Yes, I have everything I need, thanks to you."

He won't stop frowning at me. "What did you come up with when I asked about what you might like to do for your bucket list? Have you had any lightning strikes of inspiration?"

"Naw. I don't have a bucket list."

"I don't feel right about doing all these bucket list items for the kids and not for you. You're the one who should be doing these things."

I cringe. "Listen. I don't want to sound ungrateful...."

"You don't. You've been nothing but grateful."

"That's what I'm saying. I really appreciate everything you're doing for me and especially for the kids, but....I really think I need to spend some time alone with them. I don't have much time....and I want to share that time with them......without you around. I'm really sorry to put it that way. I don't want to offend you....but that's what I really need. I can't spend the time with them that I need to if you're always ar ound."

He frowns again. "That's what I've been trying to do. I've been trying to keep my distance."

"I know and I'm grateful for that...." I flinch again. "I'm really sorry."

"Will you stop saying that? I want to help you—whatever that means. If you want time alone with them, then I have no problem with that. I didn't bring you here so I could move in on your family. God knows I'll have all the time in the world alone with them once you aren't around anymore."

I look away. I really hate talking about that, but I have to. I have to start facing up to the inevitable reality.

I see myself getting tired and light-headed a lot more often. I can't do much in the way of exerting myself—not the way I used to. The weakness and fatigue is becoming more obvious by the day.

He reads my mind. "So....about your bucket list....."

I snort. "What bucket list?"

"Don't tell me there isn't at least something you want to do. Come on. Spill your guts."

"I mean....I had a lot of wild fantasies when I was young about doing things like climbing Mount Everest and stuff like that, but nothing like that could happen now."

"Is it because of the money? You know I would pay for it. I don't want you to die with any regrets or unfulfilled dreams."

I wince again. I can't look at him. My vision swims with tears and my voice cracks with anguish. "I just want.....I just want to see my children grow up. That's always been my dream—to see them married with children of their own—and to be a grandmother—and to go to their college graduations—and be all proud of their achievements and what wonderful people they are. That won't happen now. Anyway, I'm not healthy enough to do anything strenuous like going skydiving or anything like that. I get tired so easily now."

He takes three steps toward me and puts his arms around me. I can't hold back tears. This isn't the first time he's ever hugged me. All the previous times were strictly professional.

This time means so much more. I cling to him and break down sobbing. I just want a life—the life I dreamed of living before this happened. I don't care about climbing mountains or going on any kind of adrenaline-fueled adventure.

I just want a life. I want to see my children grow up and to be there to love them every day while they're doing it. Is that too much to ask?

Chapter 8: Jackson

My new assistant Devin comes into my home office and hands me a stack of file folders. "These are all the production analysis reports you asked for—all except the Silver Eagle Mine. The managers haven't turned in their report yet."

I frown up at him. "That's weird. They've never missed a deadline before."

He shrugs. "Do you want me to call them and follow it up?"

"No, I'll do that. Production analysis reports are one of their KPIs. I might have to crack a few heads if they're falling off on that."

He grins at me. "I'm going to go back to the office and finish work on that acquisition proposal for the Rocking Horse Mine. Okay?"

"Sure," I reply over my shoulder. "I'm going into the office tomorrow, so I'll talk to you then."

He leaves and I start turning the pages of all the reports in front of me. None of them tell me anything I need to be concerned about. The Silver Eagle not turning in its report on time—that does concern me. I need to do something about that.

I get on my computer and look up the contact phone number for the general manager. His name is Iyasu Batifi. The mine is in the Central African Republic, so maybe they had some unforeseen circumstance that interfered with him sending the report on time.

The deadline for the report was more than two weeks ago. He should have turned it in by now even if something prevented him from turning it in on time.

I stare at his name with the phone number underneath it. Something stops me from calling him and demanding an explanation.

I wouldn't normally hesitate to call any of my subordinates on the carpet for something like this. I need to know the reason even if it's something that was beyond his control.

Why do I hesitate now? I take my phone out of my pocket, but something still holds me back.

McKenna appears in my doorway right at that moment. "Do you have a minute?" she blurts out. "I really need to talk to you."

"Sure. Come on in." I put my phone down. I need to think about this before I make a decision anyway.

I lean back in my chair while she sits down across from me. She perches on the edge of the seat, smashes her hands between her knees, and looks everywhere but at me.

"What's up?" I ask.

"I just...." She flaps her hands in agitation. "I just don't know about all of this. I'm....I'm having a really hard time accepting.....all of this..."

I relax. So it's that again.

"You know...." she stammers. "I grew up believing in hard work.... .and paying my own way.....and not expecting other people to give me handouts...."

"You aren't taking handouts. You've always worked extremely hard for me. No one understands that better than I do."

She waves that away. "I just can't accept that you're spending all this money on me and my children—and yesterday you even said you would pay for me to go climb Mount Everest for Christ's sake...."

"I would pay for it. I would do it in a heartbeat—and I would climb it with you if you let me. I'm not going to let you go to a homeless shelter or anything like that so don't even insult me by suggesting it. Jesus, McKenna. I could never let your children go through that."

"I know! I'm just....." She passes her hand across her eyes. "I'm just struggling with it all, you know? I can't get my head around it. I know I need help...It's just really hard to accept it. It was hard to accept help even before this happened—from anyone—and now you're doing so much more. I can't even grasp everything you're doing."

I compress my lips. "Listen. I didn't want to say this before because I didn't want to upset you by making it seem like I was making decisions for your children that you didn't agree with. I just want you to know that, even if you left and walked away right now, if you really did take your kids to a homeless shelter right now—today—I will still go ahead with my plan to support them after you die. I'm not going to let them fall off a cliff into the system. That is just never going to happen. If you can't accept that now, then I'll just have to wait until after you're gone—but I'm going to do it anyway."

"I don't know if I can live with that!" she exclaims. "I don't even know how to think about someone doing something like that."

"At least accept that I'm doing it for the right reasons. At least accept that I'm doing it because I want what's best for them and I'm not doing it to be some kind of creepy, stalker, sex offender that is trying to get hold of your children."

"I know that! I would never think that. It's just....I don't know if I could accept that from someone I wasn't in a relationship with.

I wouldn't feel comfortable accepting it from someone I *was* in a relationship with."

"Look. I care about you and I'm really starting to care about your children. They deserve the best and they deserve to have someone in their corner who goes to bat for them after you're gone. That's all I'm trying to do. I have no expectations that anything will ever happen between us. I wasn't trying to imply that or even thinking that. I want to make that clear right now."

"I know that."

I raise my hands. "Okay. As long as we're clear on that, then I don't see any problem with continuing the situation for what it is. It isn't like someone else was using the lake house before you moved into it. It doesn't cost me anything for you to live there. So far, I've spent a few dollars on groceries. That's all."

"A few?" She snorts at me. "I think it was a little more than that."

"So what if it was? You worked for me for years. We have a relationship even if it isn't a romantic one. I wouldn't let a total stranger go through what you're going through without trying to at least help them. I wouldn't let it happen to someone I know, someone I care about, and someone who has been helping me for years. I wouldn't be anywhere near as well off now without your help."

She makes a face. "That's nonsense, Jackson, and we both know it. I was your assistant—nothing more. I didn't get you where you are. You did that all by yourself."

"I'm saying you helped me. You helped me a lot—maybe a lot more than you realized. At least let me reciprocate in some small way even if I can't fix the problem entirely."

"This isn't small. It isn't a small way—and I'm not talking about the groceries. You're talking about putting my kids through school and becoming their guardian and setting them up with trust funds!"

I lean across the desk and take her hand. "Just let me help you. If you can't do it for yourself, then let me do it for your children. They deserve that. They don't deserve to lose everything else in their lives when they're already losing you. Going into the foster system would wreck them. You know that isn't right. I'm not asking for anything other than that. Just let me help them. It doesn't mean anything between us."

She looks down at my hand holding hers. I hope she doesn't think I mean anything by that. "Fine," she mumbles. "I'm really grateful."

"I know you are. You don't have to keep saying that."

Her eyes shoot up to mine. "You're a prince, Jackson. You're the best man I've ever known."

I shrug that away. "I'm just trying to make a living."

She stares at me way too closely. I can't read her expression.

Without warning, she points to my computer screen. "The Silver Eagle Mine is on a limited internet provider system that restricts access to certain websites and traffic. Iyasu Batifi isn't allowed to send PDFs over a certain file size via email, so he always submits his production analysis reports through the Metcalf Mining Google Drive page. You might want to check that before you call him. It will be in the production analysis report folder under this year. It should be the only file in there until Devin loads all the other reports into the folder."

She walks out of the office without another word of explanation. I frown at the screen and then click over to the Google Drive page. Sure enough, Iyasu Batifi's report is in there and the date is three days before the deadline. I should have known he wouldn't miss a deadline.

McKenna always gave me the reports in the past—the same way Devin gave me the reports just now. She must have been in the habit of retrieving the file, printing it off, and giving it to me along with all the others. That's why I never knew about Iyasu Batifi submitting it through another platform.

I stare at the computer for another long moment of thought. She did things like this all the time when she worked for me. She was always on top of it and always gave me critical information I needed at exactly the right moment when I needed it.

She has no earthly clue how valuable she was as my assistant. She thinks of herself as some kind of glorified secretary or maybe a filing clerk when she was my righthand woman for years.

Now I have to start all over with someone who doesn't have her expertise. She knows me better than anyone. She knows my business. She knows what I need and when I need it. I'll probably never be able to replace her and that's my loss.

Chapter 9: McKenna

I bend over to check the temperature in the oven. I'm just adjusting the temperature dial when Jackson knocks on the doorjamb next to the deck. "Is it safe to enter the haunted house?" he asks.

I smile at him. "I hope you brought your wooden stakes, garlic ropes, and holy water."

The kids come barreling downstairs in answer to my questions. They grab Jackson and drag him into the house.

They start talking to him about everything they've been doing in school and everything they want to do on the weekend.

"Mom said we can go to Coney Island!" Alvin blurts out. "We've never been before! Isn't that great?!"

Jackson raises his eyebrows. "You've never been to Coney Island? Well, you have to go. That's something everyone should do at least once in their lives."

I shoot him a look over the kitchen counter while I keep working to make dinner. This is the first time he's come over for dinner since that first night. Now I'm the one who's cooking. I want to impress him, so I'm making Mexican food.

The kids interrogate Jackson about all the rides at Coney Island.

"What else is there to do?" Evie asks.

"We could go see the Statue of Liberty," Jackson suggests.

"Yeah!" Alvin exclaims. "That would be great."

"I was thinking we could go out on a bigger boat," Jackson goes on. "Something that would take us out onto the open ocean instead of just this small lake. Would you like that?"

"Yeah!" Alvin bursts out in excited laughter. "That sounds awesome!"

"I don't want to go out in a boat," Evie interjects. "I want to see the pyramids."

Jackson snorts. "We might have to save that for one of your summer vacations."

"And it isn't like you can ride an even bigger horse, either," Alvin points out. "There is nothing bigger than a horse."

"Sure, there is," Jackson tells him. "There are elephants....and camels. People ride on them all the time."

"Not around here," Alvin points out. "You would have to travel around the world for that."

"Then we'll travel around the world. Who would stop us?"

I don't get involved in the conversation. I don't like to think about the fact that he's talking about the future—the time after I die.

He wouldn't take me around the world to see the pyramids or ride elephants. He plans to save that for afterward—when he's alone with my children.

I don't like to think about someone else planning to raise them in my place. That's exactly what he's planning to do. I should revolt against that—and I do revolt against it. I want to kill someone for letting this happen.

I can't interfere in that. He's doing the right thing for all of us. I have to let him.

He doesn't mention it, either. He doesn't mention that they're telling him all their bucket list items when I'm the one who's dying. They aren't dying. They don't need to complete their bucket lists. They're just kids.

I try not to see him casting glances in my direction while he talks to the kids. They don't notice anything, not even about how quiet I'm being.

I set the table and call everyone over to eat. Jackson raises his eyebrows when he sees the food. "Holy Mother of God! What in the world did I just walk into?"

Alvin frowns at him. "What's wrong? Mom cooks like this all the time."

"Then she's been holding out on me," Jackson replies. "I feel cheated."

I stifle laughter and we all sit down. Jackson starts serving the food. The kids and I all stare at him. "Aren't you going to say grace?" Evie asks.

Jackson does a double take. "Huh? Do you really want me to?"

"Sure," Alvin tells him. "That's why we invited you over."

"You....you invited me over....to say grace?" Jackson looks back and forth between me and the kids. "I find that hard to believe."

"We invited you over for your charming presence," I tell him. "Go ahead and say it. We want you to."

He clears his throat, shifts his weight in his chair, and bows his head to say grace. All three of us say, "Amen," and he goes back to serving the food.

He pretends that didn't just happen. "So how's school going?" he asks.

Alvin and Evie exchange glances. "Who are you asking—me or Alvin?" Evie asks.

"Both of you. You made the mistake of breaking the silence, so you can answer first."

"School is boring," Alvin grumbles. "Why do they make us go anyway?"

Jackson grins at him. Jackson doesn't remind the boy that he actually wanted to go to school. Alvin could have stayed home around the clock. He's going to school because he wants to.

"My teacher almost got fired the other day," Evie chimes in.

Jackson almost chokes on his food. "What happened?"

"We're running a raffle to raise money for new science equipment. We keep the money in a cashbox in the teacher's desk. The principal walked in on the teacher trying to break into the cashbox."

"Wow. That's bad," Jackson remarks. "Why didn't the principal fire her—or him—or whoever it is?"

"It's a her and the teacher said she was trying to straighten the hinge because it got bent."

Jackson frowns. "Are you sure that isn't what she was trying to do? Maybe the hinge really was bent."

"No, it wasn't. She really was trying to break in and steal the money."

"How can you be sure?" Jackson asks.

"Because me and some of the other kids have caught her doing it before—and some of the money went missing when she's the only one who has the key to the box. We keep a tally of how much we bring in and then we work it out as a class to keep a running total of how much money we've raised. We started to notice the numbers not adding up, but the teacher would always mess with the addition when we worked on it in class. We started keeping a separate account to keep track of it to prove she was taking the money."

"Wow," Jackson exclaims. "That sounds really bad. Did you tell the principal what you found out?"

"Yeah, we showed her our account, but she said we must have made a mistake and we needed more evidence before she could actually fire a teacher. She said the state teacher's union is really powerful and they would sue the school if they fired a teacher for no reason."

"So what are you going to do?"

"We set up a hidden camera in the classroom to catch her in the act."

Now Jackson really does choke on his food. He has to grab his napkin and cover his mouth while he pulls himself together.

"I think I need you to come and work for my company, Evie," he tells her.

She makes a face. "That teacher is rotten to the core. Someone needs to expose her for what she is."

"So who's involved in this clandestine investigation of yours?" Jackson asks. "How many other kids are investigating her besides you?"

Evie counts off on her fingers. "There's me, Sabrina, Wendell, Eric, Patrick, Tom, Archer, Phoenix, Paul, Honor, Kayleigh, and Briar-Rose. So twelve kids all together."

"Wow. That's a lot."

She nods. "We all want to get rid of her so we can get a real teacher—and we all stopped bringing in our money for the fundraiser. We give our money to Mr. Watson now. He knows about our investigation and he's helping us by keeping our money for us."

"So.....so other teachers know about this?"

She nods again. "He isn't the only one."

Jackson shakes his head. "I'm really impressed." He turns to me. "Did you know about this?"

I shrug. "She's talked about it before. I hadn't heard that the teacher got caught trying to jimmy the lock."

"We took pictures of the hinges to prove they weren't bent," Evie interrupts. "That was a lie."

Jackson bows over his plate. "Maybe you should consider joining the Police Force—or the FBI."

She bursts into a grin. "I want to join Interpol."

His head shoots up. "You want to join...Interpol."

She grins from ear to ear and nods. Alvin groans. "Oh, please. Not this again."

Jackson turns to him. "What do you want to be when you grow up, Alvin? Something tells me being a pirate on the high seas isn't what your mother had in mind for you."

Alvin laughs. "Good idea."

"He wants to be a marine biologist instead," Evie interjects.

"Really?" Jackson asks. "That sounds fascinating."

"Actually I want to be a marine vulcanologist," Alvin corrects. "I want to be one of those people who uses satellite imaging to map the ocean floor and tell where the next volcanic eruption is going to come from. Did you know that the eruption of Krakatoa caused a tsunami that was recorded in London? Can you believe that? The eruption happened in Java and the tsunami made it all the way around the world to London! That's incredible."

"It is incredible, especially when you consider how many land masses are in the way to slow the tsunami down," Jackson agrees. "Just think. The tsunami had to travel around Cape Horn and the Cape of Good Hope and then all the way back up the Atlantic to make it that far. That is one hell of a big tsunami."

"I know!" Alvin bursts out in laughter again that someone appreciates his interest.

"I use vulcanologists in my work, too," Jackson tells him.

Alvin freezes with his mouth open. "No, you don't."

Jackson nods. "I'm in the mining industry. We have to check to see if we're risking hitting any underground lava pockets before we start digging a new mine—or if any of the lava flows are in danger of coming near mines we already have. We have to monitor for seismic shifts and whether we would be in danger of setting off any earthquakes or anything like that by drilling or digging in certain spots. Vulcanology is a very important part of what we do."

"Whoa!" Alvin breathes. "That is so cool!"

"Vulcanology—seriously?" Evie rolls her eyes. "Boring! I'm going to be investigating murders and international crime. That's way more interesting."

"Who gives a crap about that?" Alvin counters. "You can keep it."

"All right, that's enough," I interrupt. "It looks like you two need to put your dishes away and start getting ready for school tomorrow."

"Jackson is still eating," Evie points out.

"But you aren't," I tell her. "If you have time to argue with your brother, you have time to take your dishes to the sink and go upstairs to get ready for bed."

Jackson chuckles to himself. I guess he liked the food. He's on his second helping of my carnitas asada.

He keeps eating while I herd the kids away. Then I sit back down in my seat. He's a guest so I suppose I'm under some obligation to keep him company while he finishes his meal.

"They're great kids," he tells me as soon as they leave the room. "You're doing a great job with them."

I try to shrug that away. "They're doing a great job with me, too. I get as much out of them as they get out of me."

"I'm ashamed to ask this because, in all the years I've known you, I've never found out what the story is with their dad. Is he still alive?"

"Good question. He ran off with another woman when Evie was three and Alvin was one. I haven't seen or heard from the asshole since."

He frowns at me. "Couldn't you report him for child support or something? Don't the authorities track people like that down?"

"I did all that. No one can find him. The investigators think he changed his identity so he could disappear."

He shakes his head. "He's a moron. Any sane person would want a family like this."

I try to look away, but I find myself studying him instead. "What about you? Why haven't you settled down with someone yet?"

"I don't know. Maybe because I wasn't looking for anyone. I told myself I was too busy with work. I never looked for anyone. If anyone came along, I always kept it professional. I never even let myself think that even though everyone else around me was doing it. I just let it ride and kept pushing it to the back burner."

I don't answer. He could have found someone years ago if he only opened his eyes and got interested enough to ask someone out.

I find myself gazing into his green eyes across the table. I always thought his eyes looked hard before—and they do. They look hard when he wants to look hard.

Now they look soft. He gazes straight back at me. Is he thinking what I'm thinking? He's too polite to say anything. He's too polite to do anything—especially after how adamant he was that he wasn't trying to help me because of that.

I know for a fact he's never thought of me that way. He hasn't given me a second thought in all the years we've worked together.

He breaks eye contact first and stands up to take his plate to the kitchen. "I better get out of here before the clock strikes midnight. This was outstanding. It's one of the best meals I've ever had. Thank you."

He puts his dishes in the dishwasher and comes toward me to take my hand. "Thank you for inviting me. You have a wonderful family. I'm really jealous—and no, that isn't my way of scheming to steal them away from you."

I find myself smiling up at him. "I know. I shouldn't have gotten so defensive about it. We would all really like it if you spent more time with us. I shouldn't have pushed you away."

"You're allowed to have whatever reaction you need to have. Just tell me what you want and need. That's all I care about."

He squeezes my hand one more time and walks out to go back to his own house. I really need to listen to my kids more often. They were right that Jackson's presence does something to our family—something we need. We all need him here.

Maybe he really is a part of our family. He really does make it feel complete in ways it wasn't before. I don't understand how that's possible because none of us noticed anything missing before. We only noticed it after he came.

Maybe that's why we didn't notice—because he wasn't here. Now the house doesn't feel right without him in it. Our family doesn't feel right without him in it.

Chapter 10:
Jackson

"Mom—look!" Alvin jumps up and down and points across the pavement at the Tilt-O-Whirl spinning in the distance. All the rides, lights, and noise of Coney Island wash over the boardwalk. "Come on, Mom! Let's go on that!"

"God, no!" McKenna exclaims and pulls her hand out of his. "I'm not going on that! I would have an aneurysm."

I laugh. "I'll go on it with you, Alvin. Just don't be surprised if I throw up all over you."

"I am so gonna capture that on video," McKenna tells me.

I grin at her.

"I want to go on the Ferris wheel." Evie points to the highest cars. "We would be all the way up there."

"I'm afraid of heights," Jackson tells her. "But you can go on your own if you really have to."

"I'll go on the Ferris wheel with you," McKenna tells her.

I gape at McKenna. "You would go on that and not the Tilt-O-Whirl? You're crazy."

"I get motion sick easily."

"So do I. That's exactly why I go on it."

"So you can throw up on little boys?"

"Gross, Mom!" Alvin interrupts.

"Jackson was the one who said it first," McKenna tells him. "You didn't say it was gross when he said he would throw up on you."

"I said I *might* throw up on him," I correct.

She laughs at me. "Something tells me you're going on it specifically so you can."

I laugh again. She has been loosening up much more since she started letting me spend time with her and her kids. She doesn't try to hold me at a distance so she can spend time with them alone.

I can only feel happy about this. I love hanging out with them. I want to give all three of them the good times they'll need before the bad part happens.

I love how close I'm getting to her kids. All three of them treat me like I'm a member of the family.

She worried at the beginning that I was giving her too much. The truth is that she and her children are giving me something so much more valuable. I didn't realize what I was missing. I shouldn't have spent all these years alone.

Alvin and I go on the Tilt-O-Whirl together. He screams a lot. I laugh a lot and collapse on my hands and knees the minute I get off. "I gotta lie down somewhere," I pant.

"Just turn on your side if you're going to puke," Evie tells me. "That's how Jimmie Hendrix died, you know."

"Evie!" Alvin counters. "That is so gross!"

I can't help laughing. "You better stay here and take care of Jackson, Alvin," McKenna tells him. "I'm taking Evie on the Ferris Wheel."

"I'm going with you," Alvin tells her.

"You go ahead." I drag my wretched carcass off the ground. "I'll see you when you come back."

They leave together and I hear them laughing as they walk away. They forget all about my affliction.

I go sit on a bench and let the fresh air calm me down. I don't feel so sick now. Sitting here alone while they go on the Ferris wheel feels good. I've never felt anything like what I feel for them. I'm starting to care about them so much more than I ever thought possible.

I see them coming down before they make it to the bottom. The carnies working the wheel machinery stop the wheel a dozen times to let people get out of the cars. McKenna and the kids stop a dozen times before they make it to the ground.

I go get the four of us ice cream cones so I have them ready when the three of them come down. They all rejoin me smiling and flushed with pleasure. McKenna grins at me when she takes her cone. "I can finally eat as much as I want to and it won't matter."

"What's next—the Coney Island Monster Slab?"

"What's that?" Alvin asks.

"It's a massive steak with enough meat to feed ten people. The restaurant has a contest. If you can eat the whole thing, you get it for free."

"I think I'll skip it," McKenna decides.

"What about pizza?" I ask. "I'll buy you a pizza all to yourself."

"No fair!" Alvin interrupts. "I want a pizza all to myself."

"You wouldn't be able to eat it all," Evie tells him.

"I could so."

"I'll make you a deal, Alvin," I tell him. "I'll get one pizza for me and your mom, one pizza for Evie, and one pizza for you. You can have any kind of pizza you want. If you can eat the whole thing, you can have it all to yourself."

"And if he *can't* eat it all to himself?" Evie asks. "Because he won't be able to."

I shrug. "Then you and your mom can take home the leftovers and eat them out of the fridge for the rest of the weekend."

"What about you?" Alvin asks. "Don't you need to take an extra pizza home to eat out of the fridge for the rest of the weekend?"

"No way. That is the last thing I need."

Alvin frowns at him. "Why? I don't understand."

"Because some of us can't eat as much as we want." I pat him on the head and wind up rumpling his hair. "You'll understand when you get older."

"We won't be hungry for pizza," McKenna points out. "We're eating ice cream."

"I'll be hungry for pizza," Alvin tells her.

"You're always hungry," she counters and turns to me. "What's next, Oh Wise and Wrinkled Mentor?"

I burst out laughing. "Did you just call me wrinkled?"

"I meant it figuratively."

"Let's go play some games."

We go into the arcades and play carnie games of shooting plates, throwing balls at stuffed animals, and Alvin and I have a contest of striking a giant hammer on a pad to see if we can ring the bell.

I hit it once. He doesn't even come close. I win a stuffed bear that I give to McKenna. She blushes and grins at me. Is she thinking what I'm thinking? Does this make her my girlfriend or something? I really wish it did.

Alvin looks so disappointed that I do it again and get another one for him. Then I have no choice but to do it a third time to get a stuffed animal for Evie.

"I'm going to need an ambulance after this," I gasp when I finally put the hammer down.

"Are you hungry for pizza yet?" McKenna asks.

"Yes, and I think I will need one all to myself."

She laughs and we head off to find a pizza parlor. We sit down with four pizzas in front of us—one for each of us. I already know I won't eat a whole one. None of us will.

That's okay. That's just extra food the three of them will be able to take home to the lake house. It won't go to waste—not the way these kids eat.

Alvin only eats three pieces before he quits. I eat four. McKenna and Evie eat two pieces each.

I combine all the extra pizza into three boxes and carry them back to the car. The other three have their hands full of their stuffed animals. We're all too exhausted to even suggest doing any of the other activities.

I glance up at the sunset on our way down the boardwalk to our parking place. This would be a romantic walk with my girlfriend if I was out here with one. I glance over at McKenna, but she's watching the sunset, too.

She looks peaceful and happy—much more so than she has since she got her diagnosis. I'm glad she can enjoy these days and she isn't too sick to function.

The kids sprawl in the back seat on the way home. I want to hold McKenna's hand, but we aren't dating and I already made a point that I wasn't doing this for that. I'm not. I would be doing everything the same way if I didn't feel this way about her.

I don't even know how I feel about her. She's wonderful. I've always thought she was the greatest. I just never thought of her in these terms before.

I can't pinpoint exactly when it changed, but it did. That's okay. I can continue to admire and support her from afar. I don't need anything else. It sure would be nice, though. I haven't thought this way about anyone in a long, long time.

I park outside the lake house and put the pizzas in the fridge while she takes her kids upstairs. I stand out on the deck watching the stars come out while I wait to say good night to her.

The kids and I will be able to talk about today after she's gone. We'll be able to laugh about how she went on the Ferris wheel and not the Tilt-O-Whirl while I did the opposite. We'll be able to talk about how Alvin said he could eat a whole pizza to himself.

She comes downstairs, steps out onto the deck with me, and looks up at the stars. "Thank you for today," she murmurs. "I couldn't ask for a better experience for my kids. It was perfect in every way. It was exactly what I hoped for."

"It was my pleasure. It's always my pleasure to spend time with you and your family. I better go so you can get some sleep. Good night. I'll see you tomorrow."

I turn to walk back to my car. She darts forward and grabs my hand. "Jackson—wait."

I turn around—and realize in a bolt from the blue that she's holding my hand. I was just thinking about holding her hand. I never would have dared—and now she's holding it.

"Would you.....stay?" she breathes. "Please?"

I stare into her eyes. She really means it. Her hand feels extra silky in my fingers. She passes her fingers back and forth against mine in a stroking motion. She means *that*. She's asking me to stay.

I take a step toward her. Do I dare even think I can go there?

Her eyes dart down to my mouth. She wants me to.

I cross the last chasm between us and kiss her. She kisses me back in a rush of warmth and blissful, thrilling excitement. I'm kissing her. I can't even remember the last time I kissed someone.

I've never kissed someone like this—not someone I cared about as much as I care about her.

My fingers lace into her hair. Her smell envelops me—and then she slips her arms around me. She slides them under my arms and her hands close on my back.

That feeling explodes my mind apart. I'm kissing her and she's holding onto me—like a lover. That's what she means. That's what she wants. That's what she's asking for.

I want to seize her. That feeling of her fingertips digging into my back—they set off a concussion in my deepest being. I have to have her. I have to make her mine. I have to love her and give her everything. She's the only one I want.

I hold her much more gently. I don't trust myself not to hurt her with the strength of my insatiable desire for her.

I scoop my arms around her waist and pick her up so I can kiss her more deeply. Her tongue lights me on fire. Adrenaline scorches in my brain when I feel her body trembling in my arms.

Her eyes drift open. They mesmerize me in the starlight. Never in a million years would I have believed she could look at anyone like this—let alone that she would look at me like this.

She strokes my cheek and her fingers run through my hair before she squeezes the back of my neck. "Come inside," she murmurs.

She doesn't give me a chance to question. She takes my hand, leads me back inside the house, and switches off all the lights on the way to the stairs.

Chapter 11: McKenna

I lead Jackson by the hand up the dark stairs to the lake house's upper story, down the hall, and into my shadowy bedroom. I shut the door and turn around to face him with my heart pounding in my chest. We're all alone in my bedroom.

Enough watery starlight comes through the window for me to see his chiseled, angular features and the hard, unwavering cast of his green eyes. Those eyes consume my soul. He never looks away.

He stares all the way to the bottom of my being. Now he knows I want him. He knows I want him here—in my bedroom. He knows what that means.

I'm holding his hand. I don't let go. He must be able to feel me shaking. His size intimidates me in ways he never did before. I feel small and fragile standing here in front of him.

I've never felt this from him—not in all the years I worked for him. I always felt unimaginably safe with him. I never once thought he could ever hurt me or even get mad at me even though I saw him exacting his impeccable standards on other people.

I struggle to breathe when I see the way he's looking at me. I can't make the first move—not now—not after I asked him to stay and led him up here to my bedroom. I don't even know how to begin with him—not even to kiss him even though I want to.

I want to kiss him again. I want to do a lot of things with him—and I want to just stand here looking into his eyes. I want him to see how much I need him—and how much I care for him.

His attention and care these last few days have been like nothing I ever thought possible. I never thought he could care for me and my children as much as he does. He gives us everything—including his massive soft heart.

That's the truth. It's his heart I want most—the heart he never shares with anyone else. I want to feel good enough to be worthy of him.

He doesn't make the first move, either. Maybe he doesn't think he can—or maybe he doesn't think he's worthy of me. I can't stand that.

I raise my hand and rest it in the center of his chest. I don't know what else to do. That one touch feels like enough. It has to be.

A shiver of energy charges between me and his body. His muscles tense under his shirt. I know what he looks like with his shirt off.

Some unstoppable power flows from my hand to his heart. I'm touching his heart. I'm touching all that he is. He's as exposed to me here as I am to him.

I want to touch him under his clothes. I want to unbutton his shirt and touch the body I saw by the lake that day. I want to excite him and know he wants me—but I can't do that much.

He raises his hand next—so slowly—out of the distant reaches of time. He slips his fingers into my hair and rests his palm against my cheek.

That touch makes me want to cry in its tender, heartfelt gentleness. I'm safe with him even as he seethes with barely contained power.

He caresses his thumb across my cheek and then down to my lips. He strokes my lips and his eyes lock on my mouth. His jaws clench. He wants to kiss me, but he still holds back.

I slide my hand up his chest to his neck and face—his precious face. I finger his hair and massage the back of his neck. I want to kiss him and he obviously wants to kiss me, but neither of us can make the first move.

We come together in some magnetic storm that neither of us can resist. I don't even know how it happens before we're kissing—kissing endlessly.

It starts as deep, passionate, soul kissing. His eyes burn into mine from inches away. He never breaks eye contact and I can't, either. He holds me spellbound—and then the spell breaks and we both fall into each other in the darkness.

I can't keep my eyes open and he doesn't, either. I wrap my arms around his neck and both of our heads tilt sideways as our tongues join in a sensuous, electric dance of pure radiant bliss.

He gathers me in his arms, lifts me off the ground, and his hands crawl up my back to my neck, down to my waist, and over my shoulders. His breath comes faster. I pant to keep up with him.

Everything he does turns me on, but it's his pure heart lying right out in front of me that cracks my soul in half. He lays his heart on the line when he kisses me like this. Even taking a step toward me when I asked him to stay—it took all his heart just to do that.

I can't touch any other part of him except his hair, neck, and cheeks. So much emotion overpowers me when we kiss like this. I don't care about his magnificent body. I want his heart. I want all the painful longing he pours into me through his lips.

His hands grasp at me in desperate, aching need. He doesn't want my body—not only my body. He wants my heart—and for his heart to be safe in me. That's what he most needs. He wouldn't come to me at all if he didn't think he could get that.

I want him to have that. I want him to have with me what he couldn't get from anyone else. I want to be the one who shelters his heart and feels all its exquisite agony when he lays it out for me to love.

I can't believe I'm even thinking that, but I can't kiss him like this without thinking that about him. I can't kiss him like this without feeling everything he's asking of me.

He lowers my feet to the floor and draws back to look me in the eye. His eyes question me and search my innermost being for the answers to all his questions—and the one question he most needs to ask.

He wants to know if I can feel for him anything remotely as deep and eternal as what he feels for me. That's Jackson.

He could never love anyone any other way except eternally. That's why he's never dated. That's why he never put himself out there. It's all or nothing for him. He doesn't even want to kiss me unless I plan to give him that.

I can't hold back from him anymore. I slide my hands up his chest and feel him shudder with deepest, barely suppressed explosive fire. It's been lying there asleep in him all these years. My touch wakes it up
.

He holds my eyes in an iron grip while I unbutton his shirt. He trembles each time I graze his skin through his clothes. His nostrils flare with the effort of holding himself under control.

I work down to his sternum and his shirt falls open to reveal the cleft of muscle right above his heart. I love seeing him like this.

I thrust my face inside his shirt and sink my whole mouth onto his luscious skin. I ached to touch him like this when I saw him by the lake. I just didn't let myself think it was possible.

He gasps when he feels my lips and tongue suck the electric energy off his skin. I worked downward while I unbutton his shirt the rest of the way down his stomach.

He's already as hard as a rock. How long has it been for him? Probably almost as long as it's been for me.

He spreads his arms for me to pull his shirt out of his waistband. I wrap my arms around his waist and kiss him around his sides, up to his nipples, and higher toward his neck. He tastes delicious.

I straighten up to kiss him on the lips, but he stops me by placing both his powerful hands on my shoulders.

He holds me at a distance while he stares into my eyes. He must realize by now that I want his heart. I want to give him the shelter he needs. I want to be the one who gives him that.

He hesitates just an instant and turns me away to face the bed. He stands behind me seething with molten power. Now I'm the one who trembles at his touch.

I shut my eyes and gasp in quaking anticipation while he slides his hands down my shoulders, rubs my arms, circles my waist, and pulls me against him. He buries his face in my neck mouthing up to my ear and down to my shoulder.

I squeal in the depths of passionate desire. I need him so bad. Standing like this with my back to him turns me on more than I can stand. I need him so much more than I realized.

He lets his energy and fury unleash just a little more, now that he has me in that position. He clamps his arms around me and claws at my clothes from behind.

He rakes his fingers up my thighs, crushes my hip in a death grip, and then grabs one of my breasts while he devours my neck from behind. His animal frenzy makes me moan in deepest need—and then he digs his hardness into my ass from behind.

He massages my breast through my shirt and then flicks open my blouse buttons fast and furious. He unbuttons my whole shirt in a matter of seconds. I whimper in thrilling ecstasy. He's undressing me. We're really going to do this.

His hand clamps on my shoulder again and he tugs my shirt down—just enough for his ravenous mouth to crawl down my shoulder. I sob a little louder. I need him to make me scream. I need him to consume me—but he doesn't go that far—not yet.

He barely pulls my shirt down before he slides my bra strap off with it. He doesn't do anything more than that to undress me or get closer to taking me.

The heat from his bare chest radiates into me from behind. His naked skin touches my back and I finally feel all the wild madness of his desire pulsating through his granite body.

He puts me down much more slowly, eases his arms from around me, and lets his power de-escalate back to where it was. He buries his face in my hair from behind and stands there panting, rasping, and groaning from the effort of restraining himself.

He holds me like that for a second and then doesn't try to stop me from turning around to face him. His eyes float open and stare at me glazed with that unchained madness of his hungry soul.

I stand before him in my bra. One of the cups sags, but it doesn't show anything but my cleavage. His shirt hangs open to reveal his muscular chest underneath. I have to touch that. I have to touch him—his heart, his being, his energy, his pure sexual power.

Chapter 12: McKenna

I rest my hand on Jackson's sternum and his eyes go unbelievably hard—so much harder than I've ever seen him before. I shiver at the sight when I finally realize the beast that lies hidden beneath the surface.

I want to feel it. I want to unleash it. I want to understand how truly ferocious it can be in its power to love and desire the object of its love.

No one knows. No one feels it. No one receives that love. Is that because no one could survive it if he did unleash it?

I throw caution to the wind, let my fingertips trail down his stomach, grasp his belt, and pull him toward me. I want to feel.....everything. I want to feel his hardness, his strength, his bestial passion unchained and untamed.

He responds instantly, scoops me up again, and buries his face in my cleavage this time.

He burrows all the way down and envelops his face in my breasts, crawls his mouth sideways, and uses his face to push my bra cup aside—the one he already freed by taking the strap off my shoulder.

My breast falls into his mouth and he devours it in greedy, animal mouthfuls. He growls at me while he sucks it hard and teases my nipple with his tongue between his teeth.

I squeal and then scream out. I have to keep quiet—but I can't. He ignites an equally ravenous passion in me—a passion no man has ever satisfied. Do I dare to hope he can do it?

He rips off and dives for my other breast, nudges the cup down so he can gobble my nipple into his mouth, and only afterward remembers to adjust his hands so he can pull the strap off.

I grasp his head convulsing in so much mind-blowing pleasure. I need him to touch me and tease me between my legs. I need him to take me all the way right this minute, but he doesn't.

He attacks my chest for a minute and then raises his head to kiss me. He pants hard into my mouth trying to catch every mouthful of air between kisses.

I stare into the raving madness of those eyes. His body vibrates with so much tension that I can hardly stand it. How will he do it? How will he finally take me? Is he deciding to pull away and break it off for tonight? Is he deciding that he can't go there with me after all?

I don't think I can stand it if he does change his mind. I need him more than anything.

He holds me like that for way too long. I start to fear the worst—and he confirms it by setting my feet on the floor. He stops kissing me and eases off. He loosens his arms from around me, lets his hands glide to my hips, and stands back to look down into my eyes.

I can't read him. It must be over. He must be getting ready to tell me that he can't because he doesn't feel that way about me.

He finally breaks eye contact, looks down at the floor, and clamps his eyes shut. "I want you so bad..." he whispers.

I stroke his cheeks, forehead, and hair. "You have me," I whisper back. "I want you to have me."

"I don't want to scare you. I don't want to hurt you."

"You won't." I kiss him on the forehead, now that I understand. He does want it. He scares himself. I use my hand to steer his head up to look at me. "I want you to. I want you to do it like that. I need you to."

I let my fingertips run down his neck to his chest, flatten my hand against his pounding heart, and feel all that energy buzzing beneath the surface. He's in there. He's right there—close enough for me to touch.

He looks up at me when I touch him like that. Does he feel it?

He takes a step forward and pushes me backward a little closer to the bed. I don't know why I thought he would attack me and body-slam me down on the bed. He was never going to do that.

He lowers himself onto his knees and stares up at me from below. I can't stop myself from stroking his cheeks, hair, and lips when he looks like this.

His magnificent heart pours out through his eyes. I would have to be blind not to see all the yearning in that look—yearning for love and for someone to love—someone to worship, someone to adore, someone to cherish and care for with all his beautiful heart.

He actually feels that way about me. I only have to look into his eyes to see how much he feels that way about me.

He takes my hand and eases me down to sit on the bed while he kneels in front of me. His eyes exploring my being feels so much more intoxicatingly blissful even than kissing him. I never want him to stop looking at me like that.

He wraps his arms around my hips from behind and kisses me, but only for a second. He eases off, straightens up, and holds my eyes in an unbreakable grip while he unbuttons my pants, unzips the zipper, and tugs them down over my hips.

His eyes command me to obey. He peels my pants off, and I lean back on my arms while he slides them and my panties down to my feet.

He removes them along with my socks and shoes. He leaves me sitting there on the bed with my shirt hanging off my shoulders and my bra cups barely holding my breasts up.

He does the same thing, clasps his mighty arms around my hips, and leans in to kiss me. My body melts in his arms. I can't even resist when he buries his face between my legs and crawls up inside me to make me moan with pleasure.

I lean back on my arms. His rising power pushes my thighs apart until I prop myself on my elbows and spread my flesh wide open for him.

He goes into another burst of primal madness when his mouth closes on me. He grabs my thighs, pushes them sideways, and dives headfirst into feasting on me.

I thrash on the bed as one wave of passionate tension rises on the other. His fingers explore me, rub my clitoris, and he eventually reduces me to a sobbing, shivering, spasming mess.

He reacts faster than I ever thought possible, lunges for me, turns me onto my stomach on the mattress, and lies down on top of me from behind. His weight crushes me in the almighty power of his arms, but he still doesn't take me.

He rips my bra down so my breasts fall out. My shirt and bra hold my arms back so I can't move.

He plunges his face into my neck from behind huffing and snarling. His body bucks against me in tortured arousal, but he never goes all the way. He never even unbuttons his pants. He probably won't. Maybe he doesn't think he can.

He eases off from that, too. I feel him pulling away. I can't let him do that—not when he's come so close to showing me what he's truly made of.

I squirm out of his hold. He lets me go like he thinks I'm trying to escape. I don't want to escape. I want to feel all his fury and all his might turned loose on me.

I twist onto my back and face him. He starts by kissing me, but he freezes when I take hold of his belt again. I don't stop this time until I pull it free, unzip his pants, and push them down to expose him.

His thick slab falls out into my hand. I can't even look at it when he stares into my eyes from so close to my face.

I clasp his shaft in both hands and stroke down its length to the root. He goes dangerously still feeling me touch him and then letting my other hand slither farther down to cradle his nuts.

He barely breathes while I touch him. He doesn't think he can send me spiraling into an orgasm like that without letting me reciprocate, does he? He's the one who said he wanted to reciprocate. Now it's my turn.

I crawl down his body kissing, sucking, exploring, and finally steer his thick, juicy slab into my mouth. He groans—and like magic, he starts thrusting into my mouth exactly the way I hoped he would.

I let my hands stroke all over his chest, sides, back, and down his thighs. I grip his ass to pull him deeper into my mouth. His groans rise to snarls and finally to tortured, broken howls as he unleashes into my mouth.

I inhale him in deepest ecstasy. I love hearing him like this. I want to hear more of that.

He collapses back on the mattress moaning and practically sobbing. He sounds like he's in pain. I can't let him hurt like that.

I untie his shoes and pull them off along with his pants and socks. I unclip my bra and throw it and my shirt away. I don't want any barriers between us anymore.

I push his shirt aside, straddle him, and stretch out on top of him feeling the delicious satisfaction of his skin touching my whole body. I grind on his prick to make him hard and then work it into myself.

He jolts when I finally sit down on him. His hands grab my hips, my breasts, and my thighs all at once. I buck against him, but he only tolerates that for a second before he rears off the bed and really does toss me down on the bed.

He rises above me, straddles one of my thighs, and pulls my body upward to meet his powerful thrusts. He lets go—for one instant before he realizes what he's doing.

He leaps away from me just as fast, turns his back on me, sits on the edge of the bed, and starts straightening his pants to put them back on.

I see it all running through his head. He's scared—of himself. He's scared to let go because he's worried he'll go too far.

I pivot onto my knees, wrap my arms around him from behind, and bury my face in his neck the way he did to me. I can't get enough of him—now that I've tasted him.

I stroke his chest from behind. He feels dreamy, soft, and powerful all at the same time.

"I loved it," I whisper in his ear. "Just remember that if you run away now. Remember that I loved it and wanted more. You're running away because you're scared—not because you hurt me or offended me or used me or disrespected me. I loved it and I wanted it. I wanted all of it—everything you can give me."

"No!" he croaks. "I can't."

I can't let him leave—not after we've come so far and so close—not like this.

I climb off the bed. He isn't pulling his pants on—not yet. He hesitates because he wants it so badly himself.

I kneel in front of him. I'm naked now and he's only wearing his unbuttoned shirt.

I kneel between his knees, run my hands up and down his bare thighs, and kiss him. I kiss him in slow, sultry, passionate, longing sweeps of my tongue around his. I don't want to rush him. I just can't let him go. He means too much to me.

He inevitably starts to get hard again, but I don't touch him or suck him. I pull away and look deep into his eyes. I want him to see me treasuring his heart in mine.

I stand up to face him and rest my hands on his shoulders. My heart overflows with emotion, care, and exquisite hunger for him—for the beauty of his heart.

"Touch me, Jackson," I tell him. "Touch me the way you want to. I love it when you touch me. Put your hands on my hips."

He keeps his eyes and head down, but he does it. He rests his hands on my hips.

"Pull me onto your lap and put your arms around me."

He pulls me toward him, but he doesn't pull me onto his lap. His raging prick stands straight up throbbing in hot, brutal need.

He pulls me nearer and buries his face in my stomach. He nuzzles downward closer to my slit and then back up. He works his way closer to my breasts and his mouth closes around the right one.

He detonates the minute he tastes it. He pulls me the rest of the way in and I lower myself to straddle his lap. He inhales my breasts one after another and clamps his arms behind my hips to draw me into his shaft.

I whine in his ears. "Jackson!" I sob.

He claws up to the back of my neck, tears off my breast, and snatches a kiss from my mouth as he drives all the way home.

He pulls off my lips just as fast and stares into my eyes gasping and panting hard in time to his thrusts. He pumps me down on his length, catches his breath at the deepest point, and lets it out in short, broken gasps each time he draws me away.

I struggle to breathe fast enough to keep up with him. His size and thickness blows me apart and I feel myself spiraling into an epic climax.

I scream once. I can't hold back. He tries to kiss me, but he's already losing control of his own rhythm. He pounds faster and harder. His eyes keep darting back and forth watching for any sign that I don't want this.

I can't get enough of it. I couldn't stand it if he stopped now. I lose focus on his face for a minute and then I really do scream out as the dam breaks and I crumble in his arms.

He pulls my head down on his shoulder and buries my face in his neck to silence me. Only he can hear me roaring, screaming, and howling in his ears as the brutal waves of ecstasy take me over.

His rasping breaths change to animal growls in my ear. His grip tightens and his softness evaporates in deep, epic, pounding thrusts that don't let me come down until he blasts his primal essence into me at last.

Chapter 13: Jackson

I drift awake when I hear something bang in the distance. I have to struggle to open my eyes. I'm beyond exhausted—and I remember why when I look around McKenna's bedroom. I'm lying in her bed.

All of last night's mind-blowing delights come back with a vengeance. I did it with her—and she loved it. She didn't lie about that. She loved everything I did to her—even the things I told myself not to do.

She wanted it. She wanted to feel how hard and rough I could be with her—and we didn't even scratch the surface. She climaxes so easily. I hardly have to do anything. I just have to do it with her and she climaxes all over me. She climaxes in every position.

I still find it almost impossible to believe that she really wants to do this—but she does. She couldn't make it more obvious. Those words keep haunting my brain. *I loved it. Remember that I loved it and I wanted it.*

I might doubt myself, but I could never doubt those words. She brought me to her room and let me take her there—to the outer limits of passion, desire, and fulfillment. I've never felt anything like that with anyone.

I've never seen so much emotion and sincere connection in a woman's eyes. She doesn't hide it from me that she cares for me and wants me as much as I want her.

I want everything with her. I want to be a family with her and the kids. I can't think of anything I don't want with her. I want it all.

I sprawl on my back and throw my arm over my eyes. I can barely move. She drained the life out of me—and yet I've never felt better.

My body buzzes with sexual energy. I could go another night with her and wake up tomorrow morning even more wiped out—but I would do it. I would do it in a heartbeat.

I want her to come in here right now, climb on top of me, and bathe me in her succulent juices. I want to bend her over the mattress and pound her until she screams. I want to drape one of her knees over my shoulder and split her in half.

I did all of those things last night and she loved every minute of it. That's what I don't understand. She wants things from me that I've worked all my life to keep hidden. Maybe that's why I never dated—because I knew no one would ever want it like that.

Someone wants it like that. She loved it. She wants more of it. She would let me do all of those things to her again. She would stop me from leaving if I said I couldn't.

That's what she did last night and she would do it again. I entertain no doubts about that.

I hear her kids talking downstairs. She's getting them ready for school. She'll drive into Manhattan with them and be gone for a long time before she comes back.

I should get up, get dressed, and slip out while she's gone. I don't want to lurk around like some kind of creep waiting to spring on her when she comes back.

I'm just planning my escape when she comes up to the bedroom fully dressed. "I'm taking the kids to school now. I have a doctor's appointment at eleven. Could you come with me?"

My head shoots up. "You want me to?"

She nods and her cheek spasms. She looks terrified. I push myself up on my elbow and take her hand. "All right," I murmur. "I'll take you. I'll meet you here when you come back from town."

She compresses her lips, nods again, and races out of the room. I sink back on the pillow. I can't let her face the doctor's appointment alone. No one would want to do that.

The house falls silent and I hear the car drive away. I have almost an hour before she comes back. I don't want to waste that time.

I drag my haggard corpse out of her bed. Holy Christ, she wore me out! And here I was worried about taking *her* too far. Maybe I should be more worried about myself than her.

I stagger up to my house, take a long, hot shower, change my clothes, and eat breakfast before I go back down to the lake house. I spend the rest of the time cleaning the place as much as possible before she comes back.

The car pulls in and she climbs up on the deck. She stops there and stares at me up to my elbows in a sink full of soapy water. "What are you doing?" she asks.

"I'm cleaning the house. Did you eat breakfast before? I can make you something."

"Don't make me anything." She throws herself down on the couch. "We have enough pizza to sink the Titanic."

I snort. "You're dying of leukemia. You are not eating pizza for breakfast on my watch."

She laughs and her eyes twinkle. "I already did—so what are you going to do about it?"

I shoot her a look, but she's grinning so much that I have to work hard not to do the same thing.

She sprawls on the couch. "I'm exhausted! I should have been the one who slept in after the way you wore me out last night."

"Me!" I counter. "You're the one who wore *me* out. Don't come whining to me. You were the one who told me to stay over."

"I told you to?! I never told you to do anything."

"Please. You held me down and forced yourself on me."

She bursts out laughing. "I think you might have me confused with someone else."

"I must if you're saying I wore you out last night. I could barely move this morning."

She smirks at me. "It was pretty good, wasn't it?"

I finish the dishes and let the water out of the sink. I'm just finishing the kitchen when I get a text from Devin. I sit down on the couch to answer it and get sucked into a whole bunch of other work communication.

I tell him I'm taking the day off to handle family business—which is true. I'm going to be busy with this for a while. By the time I look up from my phone, McKenna is sound asleep on the couch.

I chuckle to myself. Ha. Take that, you insatiable little succubus. You think I wore you out? I can do a lot worse than that.

I go up to my house and bring my car down while she sleeps. I have to wake her up in time to leave for the appointment.

I put her in the passenger seat and set off driving to Manhattan while she pulls herself together and straightens her hair and makeup in the visor mirror.

I park in front of the doctor's office and catch her shooting me another terrified glance. I clasp her hand. "Hey! Everything's gonna be all right. It can't possibly get any worse than it already is, can it?"

She nods, but I can already see her spiraling off into mindless terror. I open her door for her, take her hand, and lead her inside. I don't have to worry anymore about acting like her boyfriend—or whatever I am—not after last night.

I don't know what I am or what we are, but I guess I can hold her hand for this doctor's appointment. I want to be there for her and I can do it better if I'm acting like this. I really just don't give a shit anymore if it's appropriate or not.

She huddles extra close to me on our way in. I give her name to the receptionist and keep my grip on McKenna's hand while we wait in the waiting room for the appointment to start.

The nurses eventually take her into the back. She cowers near me and doesn't let go of my hand. She doesn't act like I'm doing anything wrong by acting protective of her. She acts like she wants to me to play this role in her life.

The nurses lead her into a side room and do a blood draw on her. Then they park us in the doctor's office to wait for the results.

I don't know what to expect except that it won't be anything good. That's the one thing I've come to realize in dealing with her. It will never get better. She'll keep getting worse until she fades away and disappears out of my life.

Chapter 14: Jackson

I find myself tightening my grip on Mackenna's hand while we wait for the doctor to come give her the results of her blood draw. I don't want to lose her, especially not now when things are just starting to change between us.

I glance up at her at the same time she glances at me. Our eyes meet and she opens her mouth to speak before she stops herself.

"What's wrong?" I ask. "I mean...apart from everything?"

"I...I don't want you to think....last night....."

I cock my head and frown. "Did I do something wrong last night?"

"No, not at all," she murmurs. "That's what I want to tell you. I don't want you to think.....because of what I said....I don't want you to think....I mean....if you don't want to do it again...."

"Of course I want to do it again. I want to do everything again."

Her eyes dart up. "You do?"

"I want to be there for you—as much as I can be. I want everything I can get from you—in any capacity. I would ask for your heart and soul if I thought for one second that you would give it to me."

"I thought...." Her eyes snap down to my mouth before she looks away.

"What?" I breathe. "Tell me. Tell me you don't regret it."

"Not at all." She looks up at me with so much profound emotion—all the emotion that poured out of her eyes last night. "You used to be on my bucket list—when I first came to work for you."

My jaw drops. "Really?"

She blushes bright red and lowers her eyes. "I had it bad for you for a long time. Then I realized you were never going to see me that way and you were totally out of reach. I mean....you were this mega-billionaire with all these rich friends and the big, fancy house and the parties and the companies and everything. I never thought you would have anything to do with me—and I was right."

I'm still staring at her in stunned disbelief when the doctor comes in with her test results.

I was right. It isn't anything good, but it isn't anything we didn't already know. She's still terminal. That didn't change after last night—as if me doing it with her was ever going to make her better.

I somehow stagger through the meeting, but I barely hear a word the doctor says. McKenna wanted me even all those years ago. She never said anything then.

I wouldn't have been able to hear it then. It probably would have ruined her employment if she had said anything.

I can't believe she's been right here in front of me the whole time—and I only woke up and realized after we found out she's going to die.

How am I supposed to feel about that? How am I supposed to feel about finding the woman of my dreams, enjoying her company for a matter of weeks or months, and then losing her forever? Whose idea was this?

I don't even give a shit about that. I'm going to love her as much as I can for as long as I can. I'm not going to let a single day go by without loving her with everything I have. I don't want to look back and think I left anything on the table.

I take her back out to the car and sit her in the passenger seat. "Say something," she murmurs when she sits down. "Are you mad about what I said?"

I can't even come up with the words to answer her. I dive into the car and kiss her. The energy between us breaks loose the minute my lips touch hers. I can't contain it anymore, now that she's let the monster out of its cage.

I grab her breast through her shirt and make her moan into my mouth. That sounds spirals my animal madness out of all proportion. I slide my hand between her legs and she dissolves in my hands and under my mouth.

All the power and insanity of last night comes raging back. She wants me. She's wanted me all along. She didn't just come up with this idea after she got her diagnosis. I'm on her bucket list. I *am* her bucket list.

She spreads her legs and throws herself down on my hand. She grinds into my movements and howls in my mouth as the climax hits her.

God, she intoxicates me when she screams like that. I'm going to make her scream like that again, especially now while her kids are at school.

I tear myself away and leave her grimacing and moaning on the seat. Now we'll see who wears who out. I won't quit until she begs for mercy—and I might not even stop then. Ha ha.

I get behind the wheel and start driving back to Long Island. I only make it off the freeway before she sits up, leans across the seat, and she slips her hand between my legs.

I instantly start to get hard and she rubs me harder down my length. She actually unbuckles her seatbelt and kneels on the floor between our seats so she can bite my neck and murmur in my ear.

"What are you going to do with that? Huh?" she breathes. "It doesn't feel like you're worn out at all. In fact, you feel just as hard as ever."

She bends over and buries her face in my crotch while I drive. She nibbles down my shaft to tease me raging hard. I barely hold out long enough to pull into the driveway. I don't even bother to drive the rest of the way to the lake house. To hell with it.

I yank over onto the side of the driveway, throw the car into park, and yank her off me. She actually laughs when I turn her around, bend her over the passenger seat, and pull her pants down.

She sighs and then screams when I rub her between her legs from behind. I start by holding her down. She loves it when I get rough with her, but she can be sensuous and gentle, too. She loves it no matter what I do. Now I know why.

I take my hands off her for a split second to unbuckle my belt and pull my pants down. She rises off the seat, but she doesn't move away. She pushes her pants the rest of the way off, arches her as into me, and grabs my hips to pull me closer.

I can't stand feeling that. I need her like nothing I've ever felt. I grab her in my arms, crush her against me, and bury my face in her neck from behind while she screws her body down on top of me.

I seize her harder, dive my hand between her legs, and rub her to dripping, screaming rapture while I plow into her from behind. She screams and thrashes in my arms. The sound echoing through the car ignites my fury beyond my control. I slam into her harder.

I realize what I'm doing, but the torrent of energy coming from her keeps me going. Her channel feels mind-blowing clamped around me in a hot, tight fist until I explode.

I have to concentrate hard to ease off and loosen my grip on her. She wilts on the seat in front of me and eventually squirms back into her clothes. I sink back into my seat, zip my pants, and drive the rest of the way to the lake house.

She goes through a million little rituals to get ready to get out of the car. I turn off the motor and go around to her side to open the door for her.

I don't give her a chance to get out. I scoop her up in my arms and carry her inside. I carry her up the stairs, lay her down on the bed, and stretch out on my elbow so I can look down at her.

She reads my mind. Her eyes bore into me from below while she runs her fingers through my hair and strokes my cheeks. "What's wrong?" she murmurs.

"I don't want it to be like that." I can barely make myself heard. "I don't want to treat you like that."

"I told you I loved it. Did you think I didn't?"

"*I* don't love it. I don't want it to be like that."

"What do you want it to be like?"

I roll on top of her, hold her in my arms, and kiss her. I let my emotion take over, but not the ravenous, brutal, predatory kind.

She wraps her arms around me and pulls me into her warm lips. Kissing her like this breaks my heart with so much emotion. I can't even stand it, but this is what I want. I don't want it to be about letting all my fury loose on her. She isn't here for that.

I ease up and gaze into her eyes. "I care about you too much for that."

"Even if I want it?" she asks. "Even sometimes?"

I try to shrug it away. "I suppose I could do it sometimes."

"Why don't you like it?"

I don't seem to be able to stop shrugging. "You said you don't have the energy to do anything strenuous."

She laughs and her eyes twinkle up at me. She won't stop touching me, caressing me, and petting me all over. Her hands explore every part of me even as her eyes explore my heart.

"I don't care what you do, sweetheart, as long as you're here with me," she murmurs. "Do what you feel. I'm sure it will be wonderful."

"Why do *you* have to be so wonderful?" I ask.

"Would you like me better if I was horrible?"

I can't explain what I mean except that my feelings for her make my heart ache. I roll onto my side and pull her onto her side next to me. We can kiss all we like in this position while we stare into each other's eyes.

I can feel every part of her body and she can feel mine. I can squeeze her breasts through her shirt and watch the delicious grimace of hungry desire flash across her face.

I can rub her between her legs even though she's still fully clothed. I can make her moan and sob out my name. I can pull her legs around me and feel her hands slip under my clothes to flood me with pleasure.

We roll in bed, peel each other's clothes off, and bring each other to the heights of rapture again and again until it's time for her to go pick up her kids.

I probably shouldn't be neglecting my business so I can lie here in the throes of sex all day, but I can't pry myself away. I don't want to pry myself away. Every breath from her lips feels too important. I'm her bucket list. Who am I to deprive her of that?

Chapter 15: McKenna

The car pulls up in front of the lake house and my kids run inside. I move more slowly. The exhaustion of spending all this time and having all this sex with Jackson is catching up with me.

The energy between us keeps me going as long as we're together. Now I feel how depleted I am—and I still have to make dinner tonight. I'm not sure I can do more than that. I'm not sure I can even do that much.

I stay on my feet just long enough to check the house. He isn't here. He slipped away while I was in town.

Maybe that's how it will be. Maybe he'll just come while the kids are away so we can fool around. Then he'll leave. I'm sure he doesn't want to give up his whole life to mess around with me.

I rest on the couch and catch up on sleep until dinner time. He's probably right to keep it casual between us. I won't be around long enough for him to have a real relationship with. I wouldn't want to cause him pain in that way.

"When is Jackson coming back?" Evie asks me in the middle of the meal.

"I don't know, sweetie," I tell her. "He's always busy with his business. He's been spending too much time away from it to hang out with us. He probably needs to catch up on work. I'm sure we'll see him again soon."

"I wish he could be here all the time," Alvin remarks.

"I wish that, too, darling, but he does have a business to run and we have our own lives to live. I'm sure that won't change."

That seems to satisfy both of them. I clean up the kitchen immediately after dinner and crash the minute they go to their rooms. My bed smells like him now. It reminds me of him and turns me on, but I'm too exhausted even to think about it before I fall asleep.

I take the kids to school the next morning and come home to find Jackson waiting for me on the deck. "I want to take you into town," he tells me.

"What for?"

"I want us to meet with my attorney. He's been helping me draw up the paperwork to assign me as the kids' legal guardian after your death."

My head shoots up. "You what?"

"It's only after your death," he insists. "Not before."

"Yeah...I got that...it's just....."

He waits for me to say something else. "Tell me now if you have a problem with this—with any of this. We talked about this. You have to tell me if you aren't comfortable with this. You have to tell me before you sign the papers. We can always change direction before you sign the papers. I don't want you to sign them if you aren't clear on this."

"It isn't that. I......It's just a lot to take in. I.....I wasn't really ready to start thinking that way."

"Do you want me to cancel the appointment? I just don't want anything to happen to you where your kids would be left swinging in the wind without this protection. Something could happen while your kids are at school and then the teachers and staff would have a problem with me coming to pick up the kids. That's what I'm thinking. The teachers or whoever might get the idea they have to call Social Services because you haven't assigned anyone to step in and take the kids if you aren't there to do it."

I look away in another direction and find myself nodding. "I....I get that."

He clasps my hand, but it's the same comforting grip he used before this whole thing started between us. He's just being supportive—like he always is.

"We have some time before the appointment," he goes on. "Let's drive into town and take a walk. We can talk about it more before you decide what to do."

He puts me in the car and we start driving into town. He doesn't make any move like he wants to pull over on the side of the road and attack me. I couldn't handle that right now.

This whole terminal diagnosis is getting awfully real all of a sudden. I'm not ready to start thinking that way, but Jackson is right. I need to do at least this bare minimum to protect my kids.

He pulls the car into the underground parking garage of the Metcalf Mining. No one knows this place better than I do.

He opens the door for me, but he doesn't take me into the building. He takes my hand and leads me outside to walk down the street toward Grand Central Station.

I know better than to read too much into him holding my hand. He does everything appropriately and never crosses any line.

He doesn't make this about us hooking up or anything related to us. He knows this is hard for me and he acts comforting and supportive about it.

We wander around the station for a while and then go back outside. We returned to the Metcalf Mining building where he stops me on the sidewalk in front of the main entrance.

His eyes drill into my soul. "You don't have to do this," he murmurs. "You don't have to do anything you aren't ready for."

"No....." I stammer. "I want to do it. I need to do it."

"Are you sure? You can take more time if you need it. You can take the papers home and sign them there after you have a chance to read them over and think about it."

"No, I don't have more time. I should do it now. It's the right thing to do. I want to do it now."

"Okay. Come on." He leads me into the building. He doesn't let go of my hand.

I see a lot of people I recognize, but no one seems to notice me, not even when I walk across the lobby and getting into the elevator with the bigshot company CEO.

We ride upstairs and go to the legal department. I can't count the number of times I've come here as Jackson's assistant. We enter a conference room where we find three of the company lawyers waiting for us. I know them all.

We all sit down at the conference table. This is the first time I've ever had to deal with these people as an actual party to whatever legal dealings they're doing. I've always been able to hover in the background as Jackson's assistant.

He sits right next to me through the whole meeting. The lawyers explain the paperwork to me.

It's all perfectly straightforward and the lawyers are also explicit in telling me that he'll only become my children's guardian if I die or become otherwise medically incapacitated.

The documents include an order to my children's school giving him the legal right to pick them up, drop them off, and otherwise take custody of them in my absence if a medical emergency calls for that.

I have no reason not to sign the papers, so I do it. Putting off the moment of making that decision won't make it easier or less necessary. Delaying will only make the problem worse and I don't want that.

The lawyers give me and Jackson copies of the paperwork. The lawyers plan to lodge the order with the school in the next couple of days.

Jackson and I leave the building in silence. This moment—it breaks something in me. I'm going to die. I can't deny it any longer.

We would need this order even before that happens. That's what Jackson is thinking. I could collapse again and wind up in the hospital. Then he would need the legal protection to take care of my children.

I want that. I want them to be as protected as possible. I just don't want to face the reality that it will happen. I don't want to need these legal protections at all. I want to keep believing that I'll be there for my children all the time.

I would have needed this even if I hadn't gotten sick. I should have assigned a guardian for my children anyway. It was irresponsible of me not to.

Jackson opens the passenger door for me to get into the car. He gets into the driver's seat, turns to me, and puts his arms around me to kiss me. "I'm proud of you. This is the right thing to....."

I turn my head aside and shake off his arms. "You don't have to do that. I understand why you're doing this."

He jolts back and frowns at me. "What do you mean? I told you why I'm doing this."

"I'm saying I understand why you want to keep it casual and you're right. It's probably best if we don't go there at all.....even though we already have."

He won't stop frowning at me. "I don't understand. What do you mean?"

"I'm going to die, Jackson. I understand why you don't want to get close to me and I'm fine with that. I'm fine with us just keeping it casual and not taking it any further than that."

"I don't want it to be casual!" he blurts out. "What are you talking about? We aren't keeping it casual! Hell no! I want it to be real!"

My head shoots up. "You do?"

"Yes!! Are you crazy? What the hell do you think we've been doing all this time? We are NOT keeping it casual! I don't want that! This is serious! I've never felt this way about anyone. It has to be real! It has to!"

I gape at him in mounting horror when I realize what he's saying. He.....he wants it to be real......? But I'm going to die. He'll be left all alone.

I don't want to hurt him. I want him. I want his heart, but I thought....I don't know what I thought.

He doesn't wait around for me to answer. He starts the motor and pulls out of the garage. We don't talk all the way back to the lake house.

He opens my door for me and follows me up to the deck. I don't go into the house. "Do you need to go back to work?" I ask.

"Is that what you want?" he counters. "Do you want me to leave you alone—because I will if you want me to."

"I'm asking what *you* want. I don't want you to let the rest of your life fall apart because of me."

"Will you stop that? I want to be with you. I want to spend all my time with you. I want to have a real relationship with you. How much more explicitly can I spell it out for you?"

I squirm in front of him. I don't know how to react to this.

He takes a step forward and slips his hand into mine. "Let's take a walk. Come on."

He leads me down the lakeshore. We stroll along like lovers—which I suppose we are.

We make it as far as a stand of trees around the other side of the lake before I get out the words I really want to say. "I don't want to hurt you," I tell him. "I don't want you to be left alone after I'm gone. I'm trying to spare you that pain."

"I don't want you to spare me that pain." He turns around to face me. He doesn't let go of my hand. "Don't you get that? I want every minute I can get with you. I don't want to hold anything back or leave anything left undone. I want to appreciate and welcome every minute for as long as it lasts. I don't care if we have a week or a month or a year or ten years. I want in. I want all of it with no holds barred. I don't give a crap about the pain afterward."

I try to shake those words out of my head, but he doesn't stop.

"This is what we talked about. That pain is what will hold me and the kids together after you're gone. Why would I want to spare myself from that? Why would I want to spare myself from any time I could spend with you? Why would I want to spare myself from feeling that you have my heart and I have yours? Why on God's green Earth would I want to escape from that or hold myself back from that?"

"I just don't know how much time I have left. That's all."

He shrugs. "What difference does it make how much time you have left? Don't you want that? Wouldn't you want us to be together at the end no matter when it happens—to know we are together and that I love you?"

My jaw hits the ground. "You love me?! Are you serious?"

"What if I did? Wouldn't it be better than dying alone?"

"I won't be alone. I'll have the children."

He turns aside to start walking again. "You would be less alone if you had me, too. "

I don't say anything for a minute. I have to straighten my mind out so I understand what he's saying.

"Are you sure you want to do that?" I ask. "Then *you'll* be left alone."

"I won't be alone, either, thanks to you, but even if I was, I would still want to do it. I don't want to let you go without filling your life full of as much love as possible."

I don't know what to say. This is not what I expected at all.

We walk a little further before he stops, turns to me, and cups both my cheeks in his hand. "I want this—and you want this. This is what's best for both of us and it's what's best for the kids. Don't fight it. Just let me love you for as long as it lasts. It doesn't have to be more than that."

Chapter 16: Jackson

McKenna sinks onto the couch as soon as we walk into the lake house. I go to the kitchen and start rummaging around in the fridge for something to make for dinner tonight, but I can't help eyeing her across the living room.

She gets exhausted much more easily—as long as we're outside the bedroom. I'm going to have to be a lot more careful with her in the future. She lets loose in the bedroom and then crashes as soon as she gets out of it. I need to take better care of her.

She falls asleep on the couch again and doesn't wake up until the driver comes to take her to go pick up her kids. I have to wake her up.

"It's time to drive into town, sweetheart," I tell her.

She takes extra long to sit up. "Huh? What's happening?"

"The car is here to take you to the school. Come on. I'll walk you out there. You can sleep in the car on the way if you have to."

I help her get to her feet and escort her out to the car. The driver gives me a strange look. I give him my number and tell him to call me if anything happens to her or the kids on the way.

They drive off and I keep working in the kitchen. I'm still there by the time they come back. The kids storm in with all of their usual noise. "Are you staying for dinner, Jackson?" Evie asks me.

"It sure looks that way. Go put your stuff away and change out of your school clothes—and leave your lunchboxes here."

They do it, rush upstairs, and come straight back down. McKenna sits back down on the couch and doesn't get involved in the conversation.

The kids start filling me in on all the happenings at school. Evie and her pals got their teacher on camera stealing money out of the cashbox.

"We showed it to the principal at lunchtime. We went back to the classroom afterward and the principal came to teach our class. She told us Mrs. Campbell won't be coming back."

"Good for you." I give her a high-five across the counter. "Another supervillain taken off the streets."

She laughs. "She was hardly a supervillain."

"You guys did great. You put together a compelling case and you got the result you were after. So who's your next target—Genghis Khan?"

"He's already dead!" Alvin interrupts.

"Oh, darn," I tell him. "What about Black September?"

"What even is that?" Evie asks.

"Never mind. Here. Take this and start setting the table." I place a stack of plates on the counter.

Alvin goes over to his mother and starts talking to her about his homework. She pulls him onto the cushion next to her and he shows her one of his notebooks from school.

I keep an eye on McKenna to make sure she's holding up okay. I want to step in and tell Alvin not to bother her, but I don't want to take him away from her, either.

This is never going to get any easier. That's the bottom line.

Evie helps me by setting the table and doing a few other chores in the kitchen. McKenna holds out all right with helping Alvin with his homework. Then all four of us sit down to eat.

"Could you come over for dinner all the time, Jackson?" Alvin asks me once I say grace.

"That would be nice, wouldn't it?"

"Is that a yes or a no?" Evie asks.

"Let's put it this way. I want to. If I don't come, it's because of some other reason—not because I don't want to."

"What other reason would that be?"

"That just depends on how things go. It depends on whether I have a prior commitment that I can't change—or if *you* have a prior commitment you can't change...."

"We don't have any prior commitments," Evie counters. "We're just kids."

"I'm just saying something could come up. We'll just have to see how it goes at the time."

"So we won't know if you're gonna be here or not?" Alvin fires back. "That sucks."

I find myself looking at him across the table—and then I glance at McKenna. She glances at me at the same time. I read so much in that glance.

She and I need to have a conversation about how much time she wants to spend alone with her children—and how much time she really can spend with her children. I might need to step in if she deteriorates quickly. In fact, I know I will.

"Do you know anything about algebra, Jackson?" Evie asks.

"Sure," I tell her. "What do you want to know?"

"I need help with my homework and Mom doesn't understand it."

"Sure," I tell her. "What do you need help with?"

"We're doing binomial equations. I don't get it."

"Show it to me." She starts to stand up. "I mean show it to me after dinner."

"Then can I be excused?" she asks. "I'm finished."

"Put your dishes away first," I tell her. "Then bring it down."

She puts her dishes in the dishwasher, goes upstairs, and brings down a printed piece of paper covered in math equations.

"Oh, I see what the problem is," I tell her. "So look at these equations right here. You added instead of subtracted."

"How do you know which one is which?" she asks.

"Well, a negative times a negative is a positive, isn't it?"

"What are you even talking about?" Alvin interrupts.

"You wouldn't understand," Evie tells him.

"I know I don't understand. That's why I'm asking."

I point to a different equation. "The final number of this equation is six, so whatever factors of six you used for the middle two numbers have to either add up to or subtract to make the middle number. Understand?"

"Yeah?" Evie asks. "What does that tell me?"

"Well, the middle number is a one, so what factors of six would you either add or subtract to get one?"

"Two and three?" she asks.

"Exactly. So you would subtract two from three. The only way you can get a subtraction for the middle number is if the first binomial is positive and the second binomial is negative. Do you understand that much?"

"Yeah...I guess so....."

"And this one that you don't see in front of the middle X is negative, so the three must be negative and the two must be positive."

"How do you even understand this stuff, Jackson?" Alvin interrupts.

"I understand it because I went to school and learned it the same way Evie is now. That's the only difference between us. Someone had to explain it to me the same way I'm explaining to you. No one is born knowing this stuff."

"Can I please be excused?" Alvin asks McKenna.

She says, "Sure," and gets up to put her dishes away. I don't draw attention to how slowly she's moving. Is it just me or did she take a turn for the worse in the last twenty-four hours?

I sure hope me doing it with her didn't make her worse. I don't know if I can handle that.

I help her and Alvin clear the rest of the table. McKenna stays on her feet for the whole process and then goes to sit down on the couch. She talks to Alvin about his homework and Evie talks to me about hers.

It feels so good to be a part of their family. I really would stay here all the time if I thought McKenna wanted me to.

She goes upstairs to help them get ready for bed. Then she comes down and smiles at me when she sits next to me on the couch. "Thank you for your help."

"I meant what I said. I don't stay away because I want to."

She slips her hand into mine. "I don't want you to."

"We should take it easy on you from now on. I don't want to wear you out so much."

She laughs. "Of course you do. Don't lie."

"You know what I mean. You're so much weaker now than you were before."

"No, I'm not. I'm the same as I was before."

"I still don't feel right about it."

She strokes my hand and then leans in to kiss me. "Do what you feel. Do what feels right."

I pull her in and kiss her. This definitely feels right.

I lean back and draw her down on the couch with me. I don't need to unload on her or ravage her body. I already know she accepts that part of me. I want to be gentle with her, too.

She lies on top of me while we kiss and I explore her body through her clothes. She turns me on, but I don't need to take it any further.

She finally pushes herself up on her elbow and runs her fingers through her hair. "Can you spend the night again?"

"Of course. I'll spend the night as often as you want me to."

"What about all the time?"

My eyebrows fly up. "Really? I would love to."

"How would that work with your other responsibilities? You have to go to work every day, too."

"I'll pretend to work from home as long as we're together."

She laughs. "Maybe you should really work from home as long as we're together."

I don't wait around to hear anything else. I stand up, lift her in my arms, and carry her upstairs. "Are you going to carry me around everywhere like this from now on?" she asks.

"Yep. Get used to it."

She snickers—until I take her into her bedroom. I put her in bed, go through the house, and turn off all the lights before I go up there to join her.

She gets undressed while I've been away. She's already under the covers by the time I get back. She watches me take my clothes off and I crawl in with her.

She falls into my arms in dreamy bliss. I stretch out on my back and her head sinks onto my chest. I let out a long sigh and settle into this deepest, most peaceful rest. She's in my arms. We're sleeping in the same bed.

"Don't ever leave," she murmurs. "Stay."

"I want that more than anything." I kiss her hair. "You and the kids make me so happy I can't stand it."

She squeezes me and then throws back her head to kiss me. Kissing her gets my blood pumping again, but I don't want to tire her out. She needs to rest and so do I.

We kiss for a long time with our bodies wrapped around each other. We both drift off to sleep.

I wake up the next morning when McKenna crawls out of my arms. She gives me a look when I start to sit up. "You should probably stay here while I get the kids out of the house. I'll see you when I get back, okay? Then we can spend the day together."

"Are you sure you don't want me to come downstairs and help you?" I ask.

"I think we should tell the kids before they see you spending the night here."

I shrug that away. I don't have a decent answer to that because she's right. We should tell the kids a lot of things—starting with the fact that we're even in a relationship at all.

She leaves and I get up to go through my normal routine until she gets back. I handle a few pieces of business, answer some emails, and coordinate with Devin until I hear the car pull up in the driveway.

"What do you want to do today?" I ask her when she reenters the living room.

"I'm afraid I won't be good for very much."

"What about going for a walk? Or we could just sit here and talk about stuff."

"I wouldn't mind going up to the stables—just to look at the horses. I don't feel up to much else."

We walk up there and lean against the fence. The more high-spirited horses run around and play. The old plodders just standing around grazing and looking at us.

"Do you have a bucket list?" she asks me after a while.

"Having a wife, kids, and family of my own was always on my bucket list. I guess I kind of let that one fall off the wagon."

"You still could. You're young enough."

I smile at her. "I never thought I would, but spending time with you and your family sure has a way of convincing me."

"Do you have anything else on your bucket list?"

"Not really. I'm happy working on my company. Going to see the pyramids or riding an elephant or whatever would just take me away from what I really want to be doing—unless I did it with you and the kids—which is what the first item on my bucket list is all about."

She goes back to looking at the horses and doesn't answer. Maybe now she's starting to understand that she and her kids are the family I've always wanted. I don't want a different one. I want this one to be mine as much as if I had been there all along.

We finally leave the stables and stroll back down toward the house. "What do you say to going out on a date with me?" I ask. "A real date—like out in public?"

She grins at me. "I'd like that. Do I need to wear an evening gown or anything like that?"

"We'll keep it casual for now."

Chapter 17: Jackson

McKenna and I go back to the lake house where she changes her clothes for some reason. She looks fine to me the way she is, but she finally comes downstairs and tells me she's ready to go.

We drive into Manhattan and I take her to Park Avenue for lunch. We get out of the car and I hold her hand on our way into the restaurant. It's busy at this time of day, but I get a rush of pride walking through the door with her.

I see other guys taking women to events, dinners, and on all kinds of dates. I see these other couples pairing off, living their lives, and getting married. That was never me. I've never taken a date to any Billionaires' Club event—ever.

This is a whole new world I don't understand. I mean...I understand it. I just haven't been a part of it since I was younger—a lot younger.

I only have to look at her to see that this is right. I want to do all of that with her in ways I've never wanted to do it with anyone else.

She smiles back at me while we wait for the host to seat us. A few other clusters of people wait their turns in front of us. I'm in no hurry. We have the rest of the day before the kids come home.

I look into the restaurant and watch a few different couples and groups at the tables. I'm just deciding where I want the host to seat us when McKenna pulls her hand out of mine and turns away.

"I gotta sit down," she husks and heads for a line of chairs on the other side of the waiting area. I follow her over there to sit down next to her, but she doesn't make it that far. She hunches over, rests her hand on one of the seats, and starts to turn around to sit down.

Her knees buckle at that moment and she collapses on the floor. I try to grab her, but not fast enough. "McKenna!!" I yell. "McKenna!"

"Jackson....." she murmurs.

I turn her over onto her back. She looks up at me through glazed eyes. She takes extra long to blink like she's having trouble focusing.

I pull out my phone and call an ambulance. I don't even care that the restaurant staff and the other patrons all pull away and stare at us.

I climb into the ambulance with her and stay with her in the emergency room while the doctors check her out. They run a bunch of tests, which means we have to sit around and wait for the results.

I sit. She lies in bed drifting in and out of consciousness or maybe falling asleep. I work on my phone in between times, but I spend most of the time watching her.

I just have to be here. It doesn't matter if she's in the hospital, at the lake house, with her kids, or if she feels strong enough to walk around. These hospital visits and health crises will keep becoming more frequent. They'll become normal if they aren't already.

She wakes up after another two hours of waiting. I don't know what the delay is, but for some reason, sitting with her in the hospital is somehow just as much a date as going out with her.

It somehow cements that we really are in a relationship—the relationship I want to be in with her.

I move over to sit on the edge of the bed with her. I take her hands and stroke her hair back from her face. "How are you feeling, sweetheart?" I ask.

"Tired," she croaks. "I don't know why. I'm just really tired all the time now."

"I think I should move into the lake house with you and the kids. I think I should be there to help you as much as you can and to handle situations like this. I wouldn't want it to happen to you if I wasn't there."

She looks away and swallows hard. "I was going to bring it up. I just didn't know how to come right out and ask you to."

"You don't have to ask. I'll just do it. I'll explain to the kids that we're together and I'm going to be there to help you and them. That's all they need to know."

She nods. I have to turn her face to get her to kiss me, but the doctors come back just then. I stand next to McKenna's bed while we hear the verdict.

"The disease is attacking your internal organs faster than we expected," one of them tells us. "Unfortunately, we don't have any treatment to slow the deterioration. If we put you on treatment now, it would only make you sicker, weaken your immune system, and rob you of the time you have left." The doctor glances up at me. "It might be time to start thinking about creating an advanced directive that would allow you to just keep her at home if this happens again. You don't need to bring her in. We couldn't do anything if you did. She should just stay home."

I don't want to listen to that, but it's nothing I didn't already know.

I bring the car around. The nurses take McKenna downstairs in a wheelchair. She stands up just long enough to get into the passenger seat.

She lies on the seat with her eyes closed while I buckle her in and drive her home. I carry her inside, put her in bed, and go up to my house to pack a few things. I won't be coming back here for a while.

I make it back to the lake house just in time for the car to show up to take McKenna to Manhattan to pick up her kids. I tell the driver I won't need him anymore and I go into town by myself.

The two kids stop in their tracks when they see me. "Is she gone?" Alvin chokes.

"No, she's not gone. She just isn't feeling good, so she stayed in bed while I came to get you. She needs to sleep a lot more than she used to." I try to shrug it away. "If she goes to sleep one of these times and stays asleep, that would be the best thing any of us could hope for."

The kids go silent and stay that way on the road back out to the estate. Neither of them says anything until we pull into the driveway.

"Are you and Mom gonna get married?" Evie asks me.

"I would love to, sweetheart. I really would. I would give just about anything to be a real family with all of you. That would be a dream come true for me."

We don't say anything else until I park next to the lake house. The kids go inside and upstairs to visit their mom in her bedroom. I stay downstairs and start making dinner.

The kids don't come down for a long time. Evie comes down first, sits across the counter from me, and watches me work.

"How is she?" I finally ask.

"She's tired. She went back to sleep."

"I thought she might." I glance at her. "Are you okay?"

She nods at nothing.

"Where's your brother?" I ask. "Is he all right?"

She shrugs. "He went to his room."

"Do you want to work on your homework again tonight? We could talk about it now if you feel like it."

She looks down at her hands on the counter. "I don't feel like it."

"That's okay. It's normal to feel that way. Just let me know if you want to talk about it."

Alvin comes downstairs just then. He's also much quieter and more serious. I get both of them to help me set the table—for three this time. Neither of them eats much. They push their food around on their plates.

I try to engage them in conversation, but their hearts aren't in it. I can't put it off any longer. "I want you both to know that your mom and I are in a relationship. We're together as a couple and we want to start being a real family—all four of us—the way we have been these last few weeks. I'm going to move in here to help take care of her and to help her take care of you—so I'm going to be around all the time now. I hope you both can stand it."

Alvin looks up at me. "What's going to happen to us after she dies?"

Now I'm the one who looks down at my plate. "I suppose we'll either move into my house or we'll keep living here depending on how we feel about it. We'll stick together—the three of us—and do our best to help each other get through it." I falter before I summon the courage to go on. "Your mom means a lot to me. I care about her as much as you do. Losing her is going to be hard for me—really hard—and I know it's going to be hard for you, too. I'm going to do everything in my power to give you the life you deserve, even if it means you stay with me all the time and you don't go away to school. We'll just see how it goes and decide what's best for all of us when it h appens."

"I don't want to go away to school," Evie mumbles. "I want to stay at my school."

"You might feel differently afterward," I tell her. "If someone asked you before all of this, you probably would have said you wanted to quit school completely. Then this happened and you found out you didn't want that after all. You can think how you'll feel after you lose your mom, but it might turn out to be something completely different than what you expect."

"How do you mean?" Alvin asks.

"Sometimes when a loved one dies, the person or people left behind can't stand to see anything that reminds them of their lost loved one. Sometimes the surviving loved ones want to get rid of all the person's stuff or move to another house or even another part of the world so they don't see anything that reminds them of the person they lost. It might be that way for you. You might not want to see this place or me or anything else. You might decide that me being here instead of your mom is too painful because you want her instead of me. Me being your guardian might feel like an insult and a betrayal—and that's okay. It's okay and normal to feel that way—and it would be normal and okay if you wanted to leave all of this behind for a while until you have some time to get over it. Stuff like that happens when a person dies and the people left behind have to deal with the loss. It's nothing to be ashamed of or hide from and we don't have to try to change it. I want you both to know the boarding school is an option for you. You don't have to feel trapped here with me if staying here would make it harder. I'm here to make it easier—not harder."

Neither of them answers for a minute until Alvin murmurs in a broken undertone, "I don't want her to die."

"I don't, either, buddy." I hear my voice shaking. "I want to keep her here forever."

Evie looks up. "Can I be excused?"

"Sure," I tell her. "Let's clear the table and work on your homework until bedtime."

The kids help me clean the kitchen. They don't talk much unless they have to. I don't push it. They go upstairs and come down with their homework. I give Alvin a super basic explanation of photosynthesis while Evie does her math homework. Then I check it for her.

"This is great," I tell her. "You nailed the concept I explained to you last time. Do you feel better about this? Does it feel like you understand it now?"

She nods up at me. "Yeah. Thanks. It's actually not that hard."

Then she shows me the new unit she'll be working on next. I explain a few things to her and then Alvin asks me some more questions on photosynthesis that he didn't get during our first discussion.

I go upstairs with the two kids to make sure they have everything they need for the night. They both get into their pajamas.

Evie's laundry basket is overflowing and spilling all over the floor, so I take it out of her room, say good night to both of them, and put the clothes in the machine to wash overnight.

I go through the house switching off the lights, shutting the doors leading out to the deck, and I go upstairs to the bedroom. I guess this is our bedroom now since I'm moving in here with them—with her.

McKenna lies asleep on the bed. She doesn't wake up when I get into bed next to her.

I lie on my side staring at her face. I love her. I told her before and now I know it's true. I love her. She's the woman of my heart—and now this is the family of my heart.

This is the family I was supposed to have. This is why I never married anyone or even dated. This is why I never had kids of my own—so I would be ready when these people needed me.

They're my family now. Those are my kids down the hall and this is my wife right here in front of me. I don't have to question that anymore.

I don't have to kiss her or touch her or even for her to look me in the eye. I can just lie here next to her while she sleeps. I already know she's mine. We're as together as we can possibly be.

Chapter 18: McKenna

I roll over in bed and realize that sunshine is streaming through the windows from outside. I jolt upright—or as far upright as I can. I look around everywhere in panic.

"What time is it?" I blurt out.

"It's ten o'clock," Jackson replies from a chair by the bed. "Ten-oh-two, actually."

"Oh, no! I gotta take the kids to school!" I try to throw off the covers. They feel impossibly heavy.

"You don't have to do anything," he tells me. "It's Saturday. The kids are outside playing around. You can relax."

I stare at him and realize he's sitting by my bed like.....like I'm an invalid or something. Then I remember. I've been in bed for days.

I collapse back on the pillow and rub my forehead. "My brain isn't braining."

He chuckles. "Are you hungry? I made you breakfast."

He stands up and brings a tray of food from the dresser to the bed. He sets the tray next to my pillow where I can get to everything without sitting up.

"Thank you," I croak. "Are the kids okay?"

"They're worried about you, but they're getting through it. I was planning to take them up to my place for the day. They can swim in the pool and play games in the billiard room and whatever else they feel like doing. You should come with us."

"I wouldn't want to slow you down."

"You won't be. You can lie around doing nothing up there as easily as you can lie around doing nothing here—can't you?"

I look down at the food. "I'm sorry......that I haven't been able to do more."

"Forget it. I want it this way." He heads for the door. "I'll tell the kids that you're awake and that you're coming with us."

He leaves while I do my best to eat. I don't have much of an appetite. I shouldn't stay in bed all day, but I don't feel strong enough to do anything else.

Jackson comes back. He doesn't comment on how much I ate or anything else about the food. He takes the tray downstairs, comes back for me, and carries me down to his car. The kids are already in it.

Evie laughs. "Are we really driving just to get from there to there?"

"You two can walk if you want to." Jackson pulls up in front of his mansion and lifts me out of the seat. "Alvin, you can be responsible for opening all the doors for me. Don't forget to bring your swim towels."

Jackson carries me into the mansion. I've been here before when he's hosted events for The Billionaires' Club and the company.

The kids lose their minds when they see how luxurious and grand everything is. Jackson has to call Alvin more than once to get him to open the doors for us.

We finally enter the pool house. It's attached to the back of the mansion between the house and a giant glass atrium full of tropical plants.

The kids barely notice when Jackson lowers me onto a recliner and gets his housekeeper to bring me a drink. He points the kids to a line of changing rooms on one side, tells the kids to change into their suits, and Jackson goes to change into his board shorts.

The three of them splash around, swim, and the two kids team up to try to dunk Jackson. He's too big and dunks both of them instead.

He climbs out, jumps back in, and does a cannonball hard enough to submerge both of them. I laugh at their antics. I wish I could join in, but watching them is just as good. It's beautiful to see the three of them bonding this way.

I get wistful watching the three of them together. I might as well already be gone. The three of them are the family now.

I can live with that. Jackson will be there for my kids after I'm gone. He already is there for them. They count on him for everything now. He's their only parent—the only one that counts.

I'm glad they have each other. I'm glad they'll always have each other. He's the best thing that could have happened to them—and to m e.

They finish swimming, change back into their regular clothes, and Jackson hangs their swimsuits in the atrium to dry. Then we all go to the billiard room. Jackson has to carry me there, too.

He puts me on the couch by the big stone fireplace. This room is paneled in dark wood with rich, spongy carpet and one floor-to-ceiling bookshelf on one side. The room has a pool table, a rack of cues, a dartboard, and a few other games.

The kids start playing pool against Jackson. He wins every game until they get disheartened. Then he tells them to play against each other while he sits next to me.

They play pool for a long time and then decide to throw darts. He has to constantly call instructions over to them so they don't throw the darts while one of them is in the line of fire.

They laugh a lot and Jackson and I laugh a lot listening to their banter and watching their game.

He takes them to his home gym next. Alvin rides on the stationary bike until he gets tired. Evie works the elliptical trainer and then the rowing machine.

"Do you use all of this equipment, Jackson?" she asks.

"Not all at the same time," he tells her. "That's just crazy."

She laughs. "I didn't mean that."

He takes them around the rest of the mansion and gets the staff to serve us lunch in the grand dining room. The room is miles too big for us.

"Why do you live in such a big house?" Alvin asks.

Jackson shrugs. "I don't know. I guess I just figured that's what someone with a lot of money is supposed to do—and it comes in handy when I need a place to host events. I don't actually live here. I have my own part of the mansion where I live."

"Where's that?" Evie asks.

"I'll show you after lunch."

The kids finish eating and jump back out of the way when the housekeeping staff comes to take our dishes away. "Shouldn't we help out?" Alvin asks.

"You don't have to since this is a special occasion," Jackson tells them and makes them both laugh.

Then he leads them to his own private apartment at the far end of the building. His apartment is a three-bedroom, self-contained penthouse suite, but he only uses the master bedroom. The others are empty.

The suite has its own living room, kitchen, and private enclosed deck and garden. His apartment is more luxurious than the lake house.

The apartment is a lot more casual and lived-in than the rest of the estate. This actually looks like someone lives here.

He puts me down on the living room couch and sits next to me while the kids explore. Then they come in, slouch in the armchairs and on the other couch section, and they all just shoot the breeze for another forty-five minutes before we go back to the lake house.

Jackson puts me on the couch there, too. He starts making dinner and the kids do their own thing for a while. They come into the room, ask him questions or get stuff out of the fridge, or just hang out doing whatever.

The atmosphere between the three of them is perfectly casual, comfortable, and familiar. None of them acts like Jackson being here is anything out of the ordinary. They act like family—because they are.

He sets us up with a movie to watch that evening and he serves dinner on the coffee table. He's made pizza and homemade potato chips. "So we can pretend we're really at the movie theater," he tells the kids.

We all kick back. This is just a normal family night. He puts his arm around me and I lean against his side while we eat and watch the movie.

Jackson and the kids make comments and joke about the movie while it's going on.

They enjoy themselves no end—until Alvin drops his pizza slice face down on the floor. Jackson has to pause the movie to clean up the mess. Evie laughs the whole way through the incident.

Jackson breaks out the ice cream after it's all over. He entertains the kids by licking his spoon and hanging it from the end of his nose. Then they have to try it to see if they can do it, too.

I start getting tired long before they finish, but I don't tell Jackson to take me to bed. I don't want to interrupt the fun they're all having together.

I actually feel better about dying now. My kids will be okay and so will Jackson. He'll take good care of them. He already is. I can fade out, shut my eyes, and let them all keep enjoying each other's company whether I'm here or not.

Chapter 19: Jackson

"Alvin!" I yell up the stairs. "It's time to go!"

"I can't find my gym shoes!" he calls back from his bedroom. "I can't go to school without them!"

"They're already down here, man!" I yell back. "Come on and get in the car or we'll all be late!"

He comes barreling down the stairs. I cast one glance into the master bedroom before I leave. McKenna is asleep. She sleeps a lot now—even more than she did before.

I go out to the Range Rover just as Evie and Alvin buckle their seatbelts. I get in, reverse, and head out to drive them to school.

"I have a parent-teacher conference at the end of the month," Evie tells me. "What should we do about that?"

"You and I can talk to your mom about it tonight and discuss me going to the conference," I tell her. "I doubt she'll be able to go."

"How do I even know who the conference is supposed to be with?" she asks. "Mrs. Campbell isn't there anymore. I don't think the principal will do it."

"Who's been your teacher since Mrs. Campbell went to Alcatraz?"

Evie laughs and shoots me a smirk. "She didn't go to Alcatraz. Quit joking around."

"Okay. Who has been your teacher since she left?"

"We have a substitute—or a bunch of substitutes. Mr. Warkworth teaches on Monday and Thursday. Ms. Laing teaches on Tuesday and Mrs. Partridge the principal teaches Wednesday and Friday."

"You could ask Mrs. Partridge who will be at the conference—or I can call the school and find out if you really want me to—or we can just roll up to the conference and find out that way."

"Are you even allowed to call the school when you aren't my parent or guardian?"

"The papers state that I'm your guardian as long as your mom is medically incapacitated—so I think this counts. Anyway, I would have to call the school to let them know I'm coming in her place. I wouldn't want the teacher or principal or whoever to freak out when some stranger shows up asking a bunch of awkward questions about how you're the most badly behaved kid in the school."

She laughs again. We shoot the breeze the rest of the way into town. I get out of the car outside the school to make sure the two kids have everything.

"Thanks for the ride, Jackson," Alvin tells me.

"It looks like I'll be driving you to and from every day now. Sorry about that."

Evie grins at me. "I like driving with you. It gives us a chance to talk."

"Yeah," I breathe. "I want you both to let me know anything that's on your minds, anything that isn't working for you, or anything you want to change to make this whole nightmare easier for you. That's what I'm here for."

"Thanks," Alvin mumbles.

"You two better get inside. I'll be back at the end of the day to pick you up."

They both start to turn around. "Jackson?" Evie asks.

"Yeah, sweetie?"

"I....I don't want to go to the afterschool thing anymore. Can I just go home after school from now on?"

"Me, too?" Alvin asks. "Do we have to go?"

"You don't have to go. I'll pick you up after school. It's no big deal."

Evie smiles at me. "Thanks."

She walks away to go inside the school building. They both smile and wave to me. They look a lot more relieved and relaxed than they have before.

I drive back to the lake house and find McKenna sitting up in bed. I take her downstairs to the couch and put her breakfast in front of her on a TV meal tray.

She doesn't suggest taking a shower, washing her hair, or changing out of her pajamas. I don't mention it, either.

I open my laptop on the opposite couch and start work for the day. I work from home all the time now. This is just the way I do business. I rearrange any in-person meetings for when the kids will be in school. I do all my other meetings remotely.

McKenna wakes up a few times—just long enough to go to the bathroom and to eat the food and drink the fluids I put in front of her. She sleeps for most of the day.

She's still asleep on the couch by the time I drive into town to pick up the kids. We talk on the way home.

It's becoming even more important that they tell me everything that happens each day. I need to know all of this, now that I'm stepping into the role as their guardian.

Evie tells me that Mrs. Partridge is the one doing her parent-teacher conference. The principal already knows about McKenna's order making me the kids' guardian, so Mrs. Partridge is fine with me coming to the meeting in McKenna's place.

"She told me to tell you she's looking forward to meeting you," Evie tells me.

"Then you can tell her I'm looking forward to meeting her, too. We can decide which corporal punishments we want to use to curtail your criminal misbehavior."

Evie laughs. "That's Alvin—not me."

"It is not!" Alvin counters. "At least I'm not having a parent-teacher conference with the principal."

"Who's your teacher, Alvin?" I ask.

"Mr. Barnett. He's cool."

"What's cool about him?"

"He's young—and he's really into sports. He's super good at basketball and he's really into weightlifting."

"Really? He does sound cool."

"You only like him because he's super into vulcanology," Evie sneers.

"Vulcanology is cool," Alvin tells her. "It isn't my fault you don't know what cool is."

She rolls her eyes and I change the subject to talk about something completely different. My superhero instincts tell me an eleven-year-old boy isn't going to agree on much with his thirteen-year-old sister. It's a miracle they get along as well as they do.

We get home to the lake house and find McKenna sitting up on the couch with her blankets still wrapped around her.

"Mom! You're up!" Evie sits down next to her.

"Where were you?" McKenna asks. "Why are you home so early? You don't usually come home for another three hours."

"We asked Jackson and he said we don't have to go to the after-school program anymore," Alvin informs her. "He said he would pick us up right after school."

McKenna looks back and forth between me and the kids, but she doesn't say anything against that. She also doesn't say anything when Evie explains about me going to the parent-teacher conference.

Evie heavily implies that her mother could go, too, but McKenna doesn't say one way or the other if she will go. I don't have a problem with her going as long as she feels up to it. She would know that better than I would.

I get busy with dinner in between finishing the rest of my work for the day. I have to work everything around household tasks, folding laundry, and cleaning up. My life has changed so much since I moved in here—but I wouldn't have it any other way.

The noise in the house, the constant interruptions—it all feels and sounds so contented. Even McKenna's constant periods of falling asleep feel contended and right.

I take my phone outside to field a call from my lawyer about McKenna's advanced directive. "Why is it taking so long?" I ask. "We should have had it in place a long time ago."

"These orders always take a long time," he tells me. "The courts don't want to rush anything in case you change your mind or something changes in the person's condition. I mean—you're talking about withholding what could be life-saving medical care from someone. Everyone needs to be protected, including any doctors involved in her treatment."

"How much longer is it likely to take?"

"It could take another two weeks or maybe even a month—and after that, you have to go through a process with the hospital, too. They need to have her paperwork on file before the hospital will honor the order."

"But that means lodging the paperwork with dozens of hospitals all over New York," I point out. "We don't know which hospital she'll wind up at."

He shrugs. "Then you should plan on taking the order with you anytime she goes in for any kind of medical care—and make absolutely certain you take her in if anything happens between now and when you receive the official order. It's critical that you continue to provide all necessary care or you could be charged with negligent homicide."

I groan. "The doctors were the ones who told us to keep her at home."

"Just protect yourself. It might not make any difference to her, but it would make a huge difference to you—especially since you have to take care of those kids now. You need to make sure nothing interferes that could take you away from them."

I get off the phone with a lot on my mind. I go back inside to finish making dinner, setting the table, and talking to the kids about their homework or social issues at school.

I have to marvel that they're both holding up so well. I joke a lot about them being the worst-behaved kids in school, but Evie and Alvin are both outstanding kids. They're very well behaved, academically on top of it, and much more responsible than most kids their age.

McKenna sits up when I call the kids to dinner. "I want to come," she husks. "I want to be there."

"Stay where you are," I tell her. "I'll bring your food over there."

"I'm still a part of this family. I want to be there." She tries to stand up.

I go over there to help her and wind up carrying her to her chair. I sit down in my place, say grace, and serve the food. McKenna sits there staring at her food. I don't see her eating it.

The kids start out by shooting her side glances and then talk to me about other stuff. McKenna doesn't get involved.

We get almost through the whole meal before she looks around at nothing, clears her throat, and rasps, "I think I better go back upstairs."

I carry her upstairs and put her in bed. She groans and turns away from me. "You're so much better of a parent than I am."

"Stop it," I murmur. "You got sick. That wasn't your fault."

"You're great with them."

"I'm just doing the best I can—for all of you. Don't be so hard on yourself."

"I just wish I could do more." She touches my hand. "I wish *we* could do more."

"We're doing plenty. You're giving me the life of my dreams. Don't you know that?"

She snorts and looks away. "I'm a cadaver."

I try to laugh it off. "Not yet, I hope." I kiss her. "We can fool around when I get back up here after the kids go to bed. Will that work?"

"Just wake me up first."

I laugh again and leave her there. The kids are still sitting at the table by the time I get downstairs. "Is Mom gonna be okay?" Alvin asks.

"Of course not, stupid," Evie snaps. "Of course she's not going to be okay."

"Easy," I tell her. "I know this is hard, but don't take it out on each other. You need each other too much."

Evie stares down at her plate. "I thought we would have more time."

"We all thought that," I murmur. "I guess it's a good thing that it happened the way it did so we can be here for each other."

Alvin looks up. "Do you remember what you said about needing to get away from things that remind you of the dead person? Did that happen to you? How do you know so much about it?"

I shrug and wind up squirming. "Yes, it happened to me."

"What happened?" Evie asks. "Are you allowed to tell us? Is that one of those things adults say is 'inappropriate for children'?" She sneers the last words and makes quotations around the words to show her disdain for them.

I can't even take the joke. "My brother died—my older brother. He was fifteen and I was ten. He was always my hero—and then he died."

"What happened to him?" Alvin asks. "Did he get cancer, too?"

"No, it happened suddenly. He played football and he was always really strong and athletic and healthy. He was at football practice after school and he fell over having convulsions right there on the field. The coach called the ambulance. My brother never even made it to the hospital. He was perfectly healthy and had nothing wrong with him before that day. He always protected me and my younger brothers. I have two younger brothers who are both close to me in age. He was much older and much bigger. We all idolized him—and then one day he was just gone. I got pushed into the role of being the oldest and taking care of the younger two."

"Did you want to forget about him?" Evie asks.

"No, but my mother did. She cleaned out his room completely and got rid of all the pictures of him. She would have thrown everything away and pretended he never existed, but my dad stopped her and put everything in storage instead." I have to look away to get the rest of it out. "My mom tried to pretend that the three of us boys didn't exist, either. She completely checked out of reality—and then she left only six months after my brother died. My dad raised us boys after that."

Alvin stares at me with huge eyes. "Oh, my God! That sounds awful!"

Evie doesn't look up from her plate. She starts out by looking miserable and then bursts into tears.

I stand up and go over there to put my arms around her. "It's okay, sweetheart." I feel my throat starting to tighten. It isn't okay, but what the hell else am I supposed to say?

Alvin watches us from across the table. Evie throws her arms around my waist sobbing hard. I rub her back and pet her hair. "It's okay to feel sad," I choke. "It's okay to cry and let it out."

"It isn't fair!" she bawls. "I want my mom!"

Alvin looks away blinking back tears.

"I know you do, sweetheart," I murmur. "I know."

I stand there for what feels like a long time. None of us is eating anymore.

She finally stops crying and uses her table napkin to wipe her face. I start putting the food and dishes away. Alvin gets up and helps me in silence.

Evie leaves in the middle of it, goes up to her room, and shuts the door. That's okay. I kinda feel the same way, actually.

Alvin talks to me in a low voice about vulcanology while we work. He helps me clean the kitchen and then I tell him it's time to go to bed.

I give him a hug before he goes upstairs. He hugs me back. These poor kids need all the love they can get. I just hope I can do them justice.

Chapter 20: Jackson

I finish working in the kitchen, answer two more emails on my phone, and take it and my laptop upstairs to the bedroom. Alvin is just finishing his own stuff before he goes to bed.

Evie has already turned off the overhead light in her room. Her bedside lamp shines under the door. She hasn't come out of her room since she broke down at the dinner table.

I need to be okay with her pushing me away or going into a depression or whatever the hell she needs to do to deal with her mother's death. I'm okay with it even if she wants to drop out of school and stay home for a year or more.

I make it to the top of the stairs when I hear Alvin yelling. "Mom? MOM!!"

I rush down the hall and find him bending over in the bathroom door. McKenna lies sprawled across the floor. She's out cold.

"I just found her!" Alvin practically screams. "She was like this when I came out of my room!"

I drop everything, grab McKenna, and turn her over. She feels ice cold and she's trembling all over even though she's unconscious.

Evie comes out of her room in her pajamas. "What's going on?"

"Take your brother and go get in the car!" I snap. "NOW!!"

Both kids take off running. I scoop up McKenna in my arms, hustle her downstairs, and stuff her into the passenger seat. I barely take the time to buckle her in and make sure the kids are buckled in, too.

I burn rubber to the nearest hospital, so no one knows us there. McKenna hasn't been here before.

I pass my phone into the back seat and tell Evie to call 911 and explain to them that we're already on the way. "The lady says she can send out an ambulance to meet us," Evie tells me. "Do you want that?"

"Tell her we're already close enough." I pull into the emergency entrance. "You can hang up."

Evie gets off the phone with the dispatcher while I take McKenna out of the front seat. I carry her inside.

The medical team here is a lot less interested in doing anything for her as soon as they hear about her condition. They monitor her and then move her to a medical ward with a bunch of other cancer patients.

The kids and I stand around her bed, but it's already getting late. I ask at the nurse's station and find out that the oncologists who will be assessing McKenna have already gone home for the night and won't come in until morning.

I get the impression from talking to the staff that they already expect all these patients to die anyway.

No one here is interested in doing any kind of medical heroics to save these people's lives. No one will be shocked or devastated if a patient dies overnight. The staff expects it.

I take the kids home. It's already almost midnight. I take them upstairs to their rooms and pay extra attention to them when they get into bed. I spend much more time hugging them and even kissing them on their foreheads before I wish them good night.

Now I have to face the empty bedroom where McKenna should be. I pick up my laptop off the floor and stand in the bedroom door staring at the bed for a long time.

I don't want to go in there. I don't want to sleep in the same bed I once shared with her. I don't ever want to set foot in that room again. I go downstairs and crash on the couch instead. Maybe I'll sleep here for the rest of my life. How should I know?

I guess I'll just have to come up with my own way of dealing with this the same way the kids will. We can always move up to my apartment in the mansion if we have to.

I wake up the next morning when I hear the toilet flush in the upstairs bathroom. I get up and start going through my usual routine to get the kids ready for school, but they don't come down for breakfast when I call them.

I go up there and find each of them hiding in their rooms. "What if something happens to Mom while we're gone?" Alvin tells me.

"I don't want to go, either," Evie chokes. "I won't be able to think about anything else."

"Okay, you don't have to go," I tell them. "Let's eat breakfast and we'll go back to the hospital. We should get there in time to meet with the doctors and find out what's happening."

The kids find it slightly easier to move around once we make that decision. They eat breakfast and I drive all three of us at the hospital.

McKenna is still out of it in the oncology ward. She lies there with her eyes closed and barely opens them when the kids and I try to talk to her.

We stand around her bed for a while and then I take the kids to the waiting room where we can sit down. We have to wait another three hours before the doctors come, but they can't tell me anything I don't already know.

"Have you considered getting an advanced order?" one of them asks.

"We already started one," I reply. "We're just waiting for it to take effect. My lawyer told me we had to bring her in until the order went into effect."

"Then we have to keep her here until then. The level of organ deterioration is beyond the point of any known treatment. We can only give her palliative care at this point."

"What does that mean?" I ask. "She isn't in pain."

"We're keeping her on oxygen. That's all we can do."

They leave me alone with the kids. We go visit McKenna. She's conscious enough to hold a brief conversation with the three of us before she has to settle down and go back to sleep again.

The kids and I wait around for another couple of hours before I just can't stand it anymore. I take the kids back to the lake house and sit them on the living room couch.

"I really think you two need to keep going to school," I tell them. "Standing around in the hospital is going to be too stressful for you. I understand you're worried, but there's nothing you can do by being there except to make it worse for yourselves. Just try to keep going. It doesn't matter if you can't concentrate or even if you have a hard time dealing with your friends. Anything would be better than you waiting at the hospital or even waiting here."

Neither of them answers me. I can't stand to see how down they are. I sit between them on the couch and put my arms around their shoulders on both sides.

"You'll always have me," I tell them. "I know I'm not what you want, but I'm gonna give you my best. You'll always be able to count on me no matter what happens."

I leave them sitting there with a black cloud hanging over their heads. I don't try to make it better because nothing can.

I make dinner for them and they eat it in silence. Staying busy is the only way I can get through this. These kids need me whether I'm hurting or not.

I have to stay strong so they can feel their mom's loss now. I don't want them to have to harden themselves by pushing those feelings away. I don't want them to have to cope before they're ready to.

We go through the motions and they go to bed. I sleep on the couch again. I'm not ready to face being alone—not yet.

I can continue to pretend that McKenna is asleep upstairs and I'm down here handling things to give her some peace and quiet. I can keep going as long as I maintain the illusion.

I maintain it while I get the kids ready for school the next morning. They go through the motions, too. They do everything I tell them to do and get in the car exactly the same way they do every other day. We do everything as if McKenna is still asleep upstairs.

The kids stay quiet on the way to school. They barely talk to me when we say goodbye at the gate. I tell them I'll pick them up and take them to see their mom after school.

None of us mentions that she might already be gone by then. Should I keep the kids in the hospital right up until the moment she dies? Should they be there to see that—or to say their last goodbyes to her? Is that really what would be best for them?

I don't know. I can only make that call in the moment, and right now, I just can't stand keeping the kids in the hospital—not around the clock—which is what I would have to do if I wanted to make sure they were there for her final moments.

I drive back to the hospital and wait around for another three or four hours before the doctors make their rounds. I work on my laptop and even hold a few video meetings in a corner of the waiting room while I wait.

The same three doctors come to see me at lunchtime. "Mr. Metcalf?" an old man with wispy white hair and glasses asks. The monogrammed name on his lab coat says, *Dr. Eldridge Allenby.*

I stand up. "Is there any change in McKenna's condition?"

"Could you come with me, please, Mr. Metcalf? We need to talk somewhere in private."

"Why?" I ask. "Just tell me if it's bad news."

He waves behind him. "Please come with me. We can't talk about it here."

I pick up my phone and laptop to follow him. He probably wants to tell me that McKenna passed away while I was out here in the waiting room.

He leads me into a side office, shuts the door, and tells me to sit down in the chair. "Is she gone?" I ask. "Just tell me straight if she is."

He sits down in the chair opposite me and levels me with a hard look over his glasses. "Ms. Pearson isn't gone, Mr. Metcalf. There really is no easy way to say this, so I just have to lay it out there and let you hear it. Ms. Pearson is pregnant. She's only four weeks along, which is probably why she didn't detect any change. Her medical records indicate that she's been having irregular periods for almost a year, which may have been an early symptom of her condition that no one connected to the cause. I don't think congratulations are in order considering the circumstances. I just thought you should know."

I open my mouth to speak, but no sound comes out. Pregnant. She's pregnant. My mind goes through a dozen mental contortions trying to figure this out. Four weeks. Has it really been that long since McKenna and I got together?

The doctor stands up and rests his hand on my shoulder. "I think you better go see her. We gave her the results when we saw her just now, so I'm sure she'll want to talk to you about this. I wish it could have been different, but the disease is attacking her uterus the same way it's attacking all her other organs. Her uterus will fail at the same rate as her other organs. There is no way she can carry this pregnancy to term nor is there any way she can survive long enough to give birth to this child. I'm sorry."

He walks out of the office and leaves me sitting there stunned. This isn't happening. She can't be pregnant. I can't lose her and......

My child. She's carrying my child—the child I never thought I would have. This could be the only child I ever have—and it will die along with her. This isn't even a child. It's a clump of disorganized cells. It isn't even recognizable as a baby. It's too small.

She can't die. She can't. I can't live with that—not now.

Chapter 21: Jackson

I stop in the doorway of the hospital ward and stare across the room at McKenna lying on her bed. She looks awful. She looks like she's dying—because she is.

She's awake—unfortunately. She sobs her eyes out into a tissue—and then the worst disaster happens when she sees me.

She bursts into agonized howls, writhes on her bed, and tries to turn away from me, but she always winds up looking in my direction and breaking down in despair all over again.

The sight of her blurs in my tears. I can't even look at her without feeling this anguish. She can't die. I was okay with it before, but not now.

I can't stand hearing her roaring in agony like that. I cross the room to her bedside. A bunch of the other patients tell her to shut up, but she doesn't hear them.

"No, Jackson!" she screams. "No!!"

I sit down on the edge of her bed, put my arms around her, and burst into tears on her shoulder. I can't lose her—not now. I need her. I need this child. I need everything that we are and everything we could have been.

I can't survive this. I can't stand by and watch her die—and take this child with her. I can't even face her with the news that she won't live long enough to give birth to this child.

How can I tell Alvin and Evie about this? I can't tell them. The thought of even looking at them makes me cry harder.

McKenna holds onto me screaming in broken sobs in my ears. She understands. She feels the same pain and devastation. She's losing this child, too—the child we could have had together.

It isn't fair! I wanted her so badly. I wanted all of them so badly. This is the worst insult yet—to finally find her and lose her—like this.

Watching her fade away into sleep—I could have lived with that—but not this. Not like this.

She tears herself out of my arms and I look down at her with tears streaking down my cheeks. I can't even stand to look at her—the woman I love.

She grimaces in anguish when she sees me crying. "They have to do something, Jackson!" she moans. "They have to!"

"Baby...." I husk.

"We have to have this child, Jackson!" She squeals with another wrenching sob tearing her soul apart. "We have to!"

I can't stop touching her. God, I need her so bad! I can't lose her. I can't lose any of them. My child. How can I stand by and watch that slip away?

She falls apart again. I can't do or say anything except fold her in my arms and cry with her. We both break down sobbing. There's nothing to say. There's nothing to do.

The nurses come back just then and want to do a blood draw on her. I unwrap my arms from around her to pull away, but she lashes out at the nurses and even throws a punch at them.

"Get away from me!!" she shrieks. "Get the hell away from me, you vultures! Get away! Don't you dare touch me!"

I move in and hold onto her while she crumbles again. The nurses scamper and leave us alone. I pivot my body onto the bed next to her so I can lie down and hold her while she cries. The nurses don't come back. No one disturbs us.

She cries for a long, long time—longer than I do. I stop after a while, but the pain doesn't go away. It only cuts deeper. It hurts too much even for tears. This is the ultimate betrayal—the ultimate outrage. This is worse than betrayal. It's catastrophic.

This child doesn't deserve to die. This child could have a wonderful life at the estate. Whoever it is could have grown up, gone to school, played with their friends, gotten a college degree, gotten married, and had children of their own.

Why shouldn't they? Whose fucking idea was this—that our child—my child—should die before it even gets born?

McKenna passes out from exhaustion after a while. At least she can stop thinking about it, but knowing this only makes the process worse. How is she supposed to die in peace knowing her death will cost her baby's life?

I stay where I am and hold onto her. She's the only person who understands. We share this grief—this outrage against life itself.

I make up my mind in those silent hours not to tell Alvin and Evie. They don't need this. Their lives are hard enough already. This would absolutely break them. I care about them too much to do that to them.

The time comes closer when I have to drive to Manhattan to pick them up. I peel myself away from McKenna, but I can't leave without standing across the room to look down at her.

I'm not okay with this. I'm not okay with her dying and I'm not okay with my baby dying. This is wrong. This is worse than wrong.

I want to kill someone for making this happen. I won't let it happen—but I won't be able to stop it.

I won't be able to save either of them and I won't be able to run away to escape this pain. I'll just have to stand by and watch. I have to take the trainwreck and live with a broken heart for the rest of my life.

I never found out what happened to my mom after she left my dad to raise me and my brothers alone. I could never do something like that. I could never run away. That would be the worst thing I could do. I might be losing my heart and soul right now, but I'm not a coward.

I finally leave the room. I make it halfway down the hall before I come face to face with Dante Helme, Lane Prince, and Derek Salazar coming the other way. They stop in front of me. All three of them can see my bloodshot eyes and my face all swollen from crying.

I can't even look at them. They're all fathers. They all know—or they would know if they found out. No one knows better than they do what I'm losing right now—except that they don't know. I haven't told anyone. Only McKenna knows.

"We just found out from Devin that you were here," Lane tells me.

"What's the status?" Dante asks.

I can't face them. I can't answer their questions. I can't even say those words out loud. She's pregnant. She's dying and my baby is dying in the other room down the hall right at this minute. How am I supposed to talk about that? How am I supposed to live with this?

I walk away from them, but I barely see where I'm going. I wind up walking toward a side room full of extra wheelchairs, reclining medical chairs, and other random equipment.

The windows on the other side of the room look out at the parking lot. People come and go from their cars. Some of them are patients, family members, and hospital staff on their way to and from work.

How dare those people continue to live normal lives while I'm going through this? How dare any of those people or anyone in the world ever feel any happiness when McKenna and I have to suffer this pain?

Lane comes up behind me and puts his hand on my shoulder. "Hey, man. Let us help you. At least let us be here for you. I know it doesn't help, but....."

I spin around fast and shove him away with all my strength. Those words blast me into a whole new dimension of Hell—the dimension of Hell where fury lives.

These three men are fathers. How dare they raise their children and fall asleep holding their wives each night when I can't? How dare these men spend even one hour loving their families when another person is suffering like this?

"SHE'S PREGNANT!!" I roar. "SHE'S PREGNANT!! DO YOU HEAR ME?!! SHE'S PREGNANT—AND SHE'S DYING!!"

I barge into the room, snatch one of the wheelchairs off the floor, and hurl it at the window. The wheelchair shatters the glass and keeps going to slam down on the pavement outside.

I don't give a damn. I don't give a shit if I wreck the whole hospital. My rage erupts off the charts. I grab another piece of equipment and throw it at Lane. I want to kill him. I want to kill all three of them. I want to kill any father who still has a living child.

I realize what I'm doing and check myself enough to throw the wheelchair into another window between the supply room from the main hospital corridor. That window shatters, too.

Lane cringes and throws his arms over his head to protect his face from flying glass shards. Derek and Dante stand off to one side staring at me in abject horror.

I try one last time to bellow out to the whole damn world that she's pregnant—and she's dying. The words stick in my throat—and all my rage dies in an instant. I can't keep torching the whole world even though I want to.

I turn my back on my three friends. I can't look at any of them—not without feeling this bottomless pit of pain and brutal anguish.

I still see all three of them even when I turn my back. Their eyes tell me more than I can stand to see. They do understand. They understand only too well because their children are still alive. Their wives are alive.

These men would rather suffer the worst tortures of Hell than face what I'm going through right now. No one understands better than they do because all three of these men live with that nightmare haunting their worst fears around the clock.

Every husband and father lives with that fear. Every husband and father lives in dread that someday he'll wind up just like me—helpless, forsaken, betrayed, and broken to the ground.

I crumple against the wall and bury my head in my arms. I can't hold back the tears. I don't care if security comes and drags me out of the building. I can't live like this.

The crunch of footsteps in broken glass tells me they're coming. My friends surround me. They touch me and stroke my hair while I pour it all out. They know. They understand. They live with that fear all the t ime.

I can't even stand up to go pick my children up from school—my children. They're mine now. They always were and they always will be—and now I have to face them, too.

Just don't ask me how I'm going to get through the next twenty-four hours with this hanging over my head.

Chapter 22: Jackson

I park my car in front of the school and have to fight down emotion when I see Alvin and Evie coming toward me. Maybe they can see that I've been crying. Maybe they can see that I'm not okay with their mom dying—not the way I was this morning.

I don't know how to be strong for these two anymore. I don't know how to do any of this anymore. I'm the one who needs help and no one in the wide world can help me.

"Is she gone?" Alvin asks right away.

"No, she isn't gone." My voice breaks. "She's still in the hospital. Do you want to go see her or do you want to go home?"

He shrugs and looks down at the ground. "I don't know."

"What do you think we should do, Jackson?" Evie asks. "You know better than we do?"

"I suppose we should go see her. You guys haven't seen her today, have you? You can see her for a little while and see how you feel. Then we can go home for dinner afterward. How does that sound?"

Alvin shrugs again. Evie doesn't answer at all.

"Come on. Get in the car," I tell them.

We start the long, silent drive out to Long Island. I have absolutely no idea what to say to these kids. I'm not the same person I was this morning. I actually felt pretty good about taking care of them after McKenna dies. Now I don't think I can handle it.

I want to run away from these kids and never see them again. I want to do absolutely anything to avoid anything that would remind me of McKenna. Anything would be better than that.

These kids' constant presence would drive a knife into my heart every day. I would hate them for reminding me of her. I wouldn't be able to look at them without seeing her and all the good times we had together.

They would see it in my eyes and they would pull away from me. They would be better off with me not around—and I would be better off with them not around.

I won't do that. I'll drag myself through the next however many years of torture taking care of them, sending them to school, and doing everything they need me to do. I made a commitment and I'll stick with it no matter what.

I park at the hospital and we go to McKenna's room. She's asleep again. "We should just leave," Alvin mutters. "Why are we even here?"

"I want to see her," Evie counters. "I think we should wait for her to wake up."

Alvin turns to me. "Can't I go home? Can't you leave Evie here and take me home? I'm old enough to stay by myself. I don't want to be here."

I look back and forth between the two kids. "Are you okay with staying here by yourself for a while?" I ask Evie.

"Of course. I'm thirteen years old."

I only nod and take Alvin out to the car. He doesn't talk on the way home. He stares out the window and broods. I know exactly how he feels.

I make him some leftovers for dinner and he takes his homework up to his room. I stay with him for a while and then tell him I'm going back to the hospital to pick up Evie.

I find her in the waiting room. I sit down next to her. "Did you talk to your mom?"

She stares down at her hands. "I waited, but she never woke up. She's been asleep this whole time."

I give her a quick hug around the shoulders. "Let's go home."

She rides home in silence, eats in silence, and goes up to her room in silence. I don't disturb either of the kids except to knock on their doors and tell them it's time to get ready for bed. I clean up the house, work on the couch for a while, and sleep on the couch again.

This is my life now. I'm a robot. Being a robot is an improvement on being a man who has bet his heart and soul on something and lost it all. I don't want to be that. Being a robot is way better.

The robot wakes up in the morning, makes the kids breakfast, and drives them to school as usual. We stumble through the usual goodbyes at the gate. I do the whole routine on autopilot so I don't feel anything.

McKenna is already gone. Part of me wishes she was so I could just stop thinking about all of this. I don't want to have to keep feeling any of this. God only knows how I'm going to deal with the kids afterward.

I'll have to do something. I can't let them go through the next ten years on autopilot—or for me to go through it on autopilot. They need a living, breathing, caring person—not some robot.

I drive back to the hospital and hunt high and low until I find Dr. Allenby. It takes an act of God to convince the hospital staff to tell me where he is. I find him in the top floor office that must be his real office. It isn't the same one where he took me last time.

"Look. Can't you find some way to release McKenna to go home for her last days or weeks alive?" I ask. "Why does she have to stay here if you can't do anything for her? Just let her go home. Don't let her die in the hospital. This whole nightmare is killing her children—and me ."

He waves me to the seat across from his desk. "Sit down, Mr. Metcalf. We need to talk."

I sit down. I don't want to sit down and I sure as hell don't want to talk. I don't want to hear any other bad news. I want to take McKenna home. I never want to set foot in this damn hospital again as long as I live—and I don't want my kids setting foot in here, either.

They're my kids now. They have never been anything else. They sure as hell aren't anyone else's kids. That makes them mine.

"What's wrong?" I demand. "What could possibly be worse than what you've already told me? Why does McKenna have to stay here?"

He leans across the desk again. "Ms. Pearson's blood serum levels are coming down—and they're coming down rapidly. Her pregnancy and the change in her hormone panel is sending her into remission. Her organs are still dangerously depleted, but she should start to recover again as her pregnancy progresses. There is a high chance she could carry this baby to term after all—and before you ask, no, there is no way to guarantee that her leukemia won't come back as soon as she delivers. I wish I could tell you that this is the cure we've all been looking for, but it isn't. She will almost certainly survive long enough to give birth to this baby. All bets are off after that."

I blink at him. "Um....what?"

"Ms. Pearson is in remission. Her pregnancy hormones are quelling the spread of her leukemia. It will take time for her....."

"I got that," I snap. "You said.....you said it could come back....aft erward."

"I'm afraid so. The only option is that we could start her on treatment the minute she gives birth. We would already be anticipating that she would get leukemia again—or she might not. She might remain perfectly healthy after she gives birth—in which case we would just monitor her levels and see if they start to rise again. I see no reason to put her on treatment if she doesn't need to be."

I can't stop staring at him. Those words barely penetrate my brain. Would it be better to lose McKenna now—or to be stuck with a newborn I have to raise alone?

I stumble out of his office and back downstairs. I can't deal with this. I can't deal with any of it.

I stop in the doorway of her room and look in at her. She lies on her bed. She's awake now. Her eyes soften and she smiles at me so beautifully that my heart spasms.

I can't keep away from her—and yet everything about her hurts worse than any pain I've ever endured.

I make it as far as her bedside. She takes my hand. "Did you hear?" she half-whispers. "Did they tell you?"

"Yeah," I croak. "They told me."

"Isn't it wonderful?" she breathes. "I can actually give birth to this baby. The baby can live."

I try to compress my lips, but I already feel my emotions getting the better of me. "But....I could lose you anyway." Tears streak down my cheeks. I love her more than anything.

"But don't you see?" she murmurs. "You would have this child. You wouldn't be alone."

"I don't want the child! I want you! How am I supposed to raise a newborn baby without a mother?"

She squeezes my hand. "You're going to be wonderful. You're kind and loving and gentle. You're going to be perfect—and there's just as much of a chance that I'll be there to do it with you. Don't you see? We can be a family. We can live our lives together the way we always wanted to."

"I....I can't lose you....." My face spasms. I can barely get my lips to form the words. "Not now....."

"Be happy about this. Be happy that I'm getting better and we're going to have a baby and be together. Don't be sad about that. Won't it be better for you to have this child even if I die? Then you won't be alone. You'll always have a piece of me with you."

"I don't want a piece of you. I want you. I need you and this child needs you."

She bursts into a beautiful, ecstatic smile. "I love you. I love everything about you. I always have. I want all of that with you—every day that we have together. I don't care how long we have. We could live to be a hundred. One of us will die first. Then these children will be the glue that holds us together and gets us through it." She pulls me closer to the bed. "I want to have a child with you."

"I want that, too, but I want it all." I choke on tears. "I don't want you to go."

I break down sobbing at those words. I can't lose her. I can't lose either of them.

She draws me down into her arms, but she doesn't cry. She's too happy about this. "I don't want to go, either," she murmurs in my ear, "but it would be better to do half of it than none at all. You said you wanted me to complete my bucket list and not die with any regrets. This is it. We both want this—for however long it lasts. Be happy with me. Let us be happy together."

I fall apart on her shoulder. I can't tell if I'm happy or sad. I'm both. I love her beyond words, but I was always going to lose her even without the leukemia.

I'll live with that fear hanging over my head and haunting my darkest hours—just like every other husband and father out there. Some men fear that their wives will get hit by a car. Others fear that their children will get kidnapped or die in a plane crash.

My phantom will be leukemia. I got nine extra months. All bets are off after that—but the truth is that it was always there. I would have lived with that fear no matter what the phantom was. At least I know what it is now.

My child. My wife. My family. My children. My house.

I'm all those things and she's right here in my arms. I don't have to worry about her dying—not for another nine months. Now I have all the other stuff to worry about—the same stuff every other man has to worry about.

I have to worry about my kids coping with bad things that happen. I have to worry about one of my family winding up in the hospital.

I have to worry about my baby getting sick or my wife having a miscarriage or some drunk driver coming along and wiping us all off the map. I said I wanted a family. Now I have one along with all the agony and paralyzing fear that goes with it.

I finally force myself to sit up. She won't stop smiling at me. Even my tears make her smile. She strokes them off my cheeks and runs her fingers through my hair.

"Everything is going to be wonderful," she murmurs. "You'll see. I'm going to be healthy. I'm going to recover. I have too much to live f or."

I can't even answer her.

"Do you love me?" she whispers.

I can only nod. Those words bring so many silent tears to my eyes. I love her more than life itself. I love all our children. I just want her—and them. I can't lose this—not now.

I just have to live with that fear—and that's what I'll do. I'll just have to get my game face on and start doing everything every other husband and father is out there doing.

They're getting up in the morning, sending their kids to school, going to work, keeping the house, raising their children, helping with their homework, bringing in the groceries, mowing the lawn.....all with the phantom lurking in the background.

I'm one of those men now.

"Marry me." The words come from the depths of my soul. I don't see how I can do anything else. "Marry me. I can't do this without you."

"Yes!" she whispers. "Yes, I will."

I can't even hug or kiss her. Just looking at her feels like the greatest benediction I could ask for.

I have never seen her so happy. She glows with pleasure—and hope. I don't know how to cope with that. I don't think I can live with that hope—the hope that everything is going to be okay. I can't face that something might pull the rug out from under me.

I don't want to stop looking at her—not ever. I want her in my life always—but that isn't possible. I only have her for a short time—one short lifetime. That isn't near enough time to look at her as much as I want to.

I don't even care if I ever kiss her or touch her or see her naked again. None of it means anything as long as she's here in front of me.

We have a lifetime. It might be short. It might be long. She might be healthy. She might be sick. She'll be the mother and I'll be the father to these children until one of us goes. Then the other will step in and finish the job.

That's the deal we signed for the blessing of looking at each other like this—of feeling how much we love each other and would sacrifice anything just for a few more minutes of looking at each other.

Nine months. That's all I can count on. I can't squander that time.

I'm going to marry her as soon as humanly possible. That's all I can do. That's all any man can do. I just have to take the rest and let the chips fall where they may.

Chapter 23: McKenna

I see movement out of the corner of my eye, look up, and spot my children standing in the door of my hospital ward. Jackson stands behind them.

His features spasm with so much buried turmoil. I know he loves me. He doesn't even have to say the words.

He doesn't know what will happen to us and neither do I. I love him. I want him. I want a life with him. I want to marry him and take anything that comes—and that starts right now.

I hold out my hand to my children. I'm still too weak to sit up in bed, but I'll get better. I already feel better just in the couple of days since I've been lying here.

This pregnancy is the best thing that has ever happened to me. I'm going to have another child—and this pregnancy is going to kill the leukemia. I don't know how I know that, but I sense it in my gut.

This pregnancy is the turning point. It's the trigger that switches me back to being healthy. I won't get sick after this. I feel that truth in the innermost core of my being.

My children hesitate to come near me until Jackson steers them into the room. I barely remember talking to them before. I couldn't think clearly about anything. All our conversations felt like they were happening in a distant dream.

I can think clearly now and see my children clearly. I clasp both of them by their hands.

"Are you about to die, Mom?" Alvin asks. "Is this goodbye?"

I can't help but smile at him and tears spring to my eyes—tears of happiness. "No, darling. I'm not dying and this isn't goodbye. I'm going to get better."

"What do you mean?" Evie asks. "How is that possible when you're so sick?"

I take a deep breath. Jackson stands there watching and listening. His features jolt all over the place. This has to be hard for him.

"The truth is...I'm pregnant," I blurt out. "Jackson and I are going to have a child together—and me being pregnant is making the leukemia to go down. My hormones are sending me into remission. I'm going to get better and give birth to this child—your younger brother or sister."

They both gape at me with their jaws on the floor. "Seriously?!" Evie gasps.

"Yes, seriously." I squeeze both their hands again. I don't seem to be able to stop doing that. "Now I need you both to listen to me very carefully. There is no guarantee that the leukemia might not come back after I give birth. We don't know for certain. I could live a long time and never get sick again. The point is that the four of us are going to live together as a family for as long as it lasts. We're going to love each other and support each other and enjoy every day and every minute we have together. We got an extension. That's all—but we don't know how long it will last. No one does. Do you understand? We're going to stand together and pull together as a family no matter what happens. Okay? So I need you both to help Jackson as much as you can—and

I'm going to do my part by getting healthy and staying that way for as long as I can so I can be there to love you both—all three of you—and watch you grow up the way I originally wanted to. That's what we're shooting for. Okay?"

They both gulp. Alvin nods. Evie won't stop staring at me in stunned shock. I guess I can't blame her.

Jackson moves in to save the day. "I better take you kids home. We can think about this and talk about it some more later. Your mom is going to take some time to recover before she's strong enough to come home. We don't need to figure everything out now. Come on. Let's go."

He steers them out of the room and comes back a second later to sit on the edge of my bed. He hugs me and then kisses me very lightly on the lips. "I love you," he husks.

"I love you, too. Take care of my babies."

"You, too." He sits up to look into my eyes. "I'm trusting you."

"I won't let you down." I caress his cheeks and beam up at him. He makes me so happy. "I'll miss you. I'm going to do everything I can to come home to you."

He barely chokes out, "I need you."

"I need you, too. I can't do this without you. We're going to make this work. I promise."

He kisses me again and leaves. Now I'm alone for the night, but I know what I have to do. My whole family needs me—and this baby needs me.

I have to get healthy and I have to stay healthy. I need to be the mother these children need. I can't die—not now. I have too much to live for.

Chapter 24:
Jackson

I keep one arm around each of the kids' shoulders on our way out to the hospital parking lot. I open the car doors for the kids to get in, but Evie stops me there and turns to face me. "Jackson?"

"Yeah, sweetheart?"

"You.....you and Mom......" She doesn't finish.

I don't even know what to say to her. I'm still a mess after finding out that she's in remission and I'm going to have this child. I might not get to keep McKenna, but I'm about to have a child of my own.

How am I supposed to feel about that knowing it could cost me the woman of my dreams?

"Don't even say it," Alvin interrupts. "Don't even think it."

She ignores him. "You won't....you know.....you won't forget about us....will you?"

"Of course not, sweetheart." My voice breaks. "I consider you and Alvin my kids, too—my first kids. You're the ones who are getting me through this—and you're the ones who will keep getting me through it if something happens to her after this. I can't lose you. You're too important to me—both of you. I'll always be there for you and we'll always be family no matter what happens to your mom."

She looks away. I dive in and give her a quick hug.

"Let's go home," I tell her. "Nine months is a long time. A lot can happen in that time and we don't even know how long it will take for your mom to get healthy enough to come home. You and me and Alvin are gonna be stuck with each other for a long time—plenty of time for you to get sick of me and decide you don't like me after all."

"No, we won't," Alvin interrupts.

"Not even if I tell you what to do? Get in the car. It's a school night."

Both kids groan. I find myself laughing. Maybe I'm going to be okay after all—and we're going to be okay after all. I can only keep going and hope for the best.

I get behind the wheel and drive them home. We go through our usual routine, but it feels different. None of us is on autopilot anymore. The looming threat that McKenna might die in nine months feels far enough away for us to put it out of our minds—for now.

I make dinner again as usual. Nothing about our lives has changed in that way and it isn't likely to change anytime soon.

The kids and I talk about school and other stuff during dinner. Then I help them with their homework again. I'm supposed to tell them to go to bed after this, but I don't. We sit up talking for a long time—probably later than we should.

"What's going to happen after Mom comes home?" Alvin asks.

"Why do you keep asking that?" Evie fires back. "No one can predict the future. You're asking Jackson to tell you something no one could possibly know. You wanted to know what would happen after Mom died and now you're asking what's going to happen after she comes home. We just have to wait and find out."

"There's nothing wrong with asking," I interject. "The question is how healthy your mom will be when she comes home. She could be bedridden for a while—and then she could have issues with her pregnancy. We won't know any of that until she does come home—but the truth is that no one knows how pregnancy is going to affect any woman. Some get really sick and weak. Some feel fantastic and stronger and have more energy than they've ever had in their lives. Some can't walk. Others can't sit still and exercise all through their pregnancies."

"That's never going to happen to Mom," Evie points out.

"I'm saying that we're all in exactly the same boat as every other family on the planet," I tell her. "See what I mean? The mother's health is a big question mark for every family. Every family has to live with the uncertainty of how a pregnancy is going to affect the mother—just like every family has to live with the uncertainty of whether one of the members will die too soon. Every kid has to live with that uncertainty. You kids aren't different from every other kid because you're worried that your mom is going to die—or if you're worried I might die."

The kids fall into a thoughtful silence. I have to finish this once and for all.

"It's the same for the adults. Every parent worries that one of their kids will get hurt and die. Every parent worries that their spouse will get hurt and die. Everyone lives with that fear. We do, too. I'll spend my life worrying about you and your mom. You'll spend your lives worrying about me and your mom dying and leaving you alone. Every kid worries about that. Your mom will worry about you and your little baby brother or sister. That's what being family is. It means you only get to keep these people for a short time and you better make the most of it while it lasts."

"I don't like it," Alvin grumbles. "I don't like it at all."

"I don't like it, either, champ. I absolutely hate it, but I'm not going to let that stop me from loving all of you as much as I can. Oh, by the way, your mom and I are gonna get married. I thought you ought to know."

"You didn't actually think we didn't know, did you?" Evie sneers.

I laugh at her. "I'm glad someone figured it out."

"When is it happening?" Alvin asks. "Are we not a family before that?"

"Of course we are. We'll be family no matter what. I don't think it will happen before your mom comes home, but anything is possible. The three of us will be together either way."

"Did you know?" Evie asks me. "Did you and Mom plan to get pregnant....to make her well?"

"Evie—ew!" Alvin grimaces. "How can you even ask that?"

"Well, you know how women get pregnant," she counters. "It isn't a secret. You're eleven years old. Grow up!"

"We didn't plan any of this," I tell her. "I really thought I was going to die when I found out she was pregnant and I thought she was going to die anyway. I thought the baby would die with her. I would have done just about anything to spare myself from that. We didn't find out until today that she was getting better."

"So....she could get sick again....even while she's pregnant," Evie points out. "We don't even know if she'll last the nine months."

"EVIE!!" Alvin roars.

I hold up my hand. "You can't blame your sister for wanting to understand, Alvin. There's no harm in asking questions." I turn back to Evie. "Technically, no, we don't know if she'll get sick again even while she's pregnant. We don't know anything—not anything at all."

"This sucks," Alvin snarls.

"I agree with you, champ. I absolutely agree with you."

"But if that happened...," Evie goes on. "If she started to get well again....she might live long enough to give birth. She might live long enough for them to deliver the baby prematurely....or something like that."

Alvin throws up his hands and jumps to his feet. "I'm not listening to this."

He races off to the stairs and disappears into his room. I take a deep breath. "I suppose it's theoretically possible that your mom could give birth or even for the doctors to deliver the baby prematurely—but I think you might have a point here. I think you're letting wild speculation run away with you—and you're trying to predict the future when no one can. We all have to live with the uncertainty. That's the harsh reality. I don't like it any better than you do. In fact, I absolutely hate it, but I'm gonna keep doing it because I love you and your brother and your mom and our baby. I'm gonna keep doing it because I don't want to miss even a moment with any of you even if it sucks and it's painful and sad and hard. That's what I'm going to do. I don't see that I have much choice about that. It isn't like I can run away from it all like my mom did. I wouldn't do that."

She nods to herself and stands up. "I think I better go to bed. It's a school night."

I get to my feet. "Good night, sweetheart. Sleep tight. I'll be here if you need anything."

She studies me for a minute and then rushes me. She throws her arms around me and squeezes tight in a huge hug. "I love you, Jackson," she chokes in my ear. "Thank you—for everything."

She races away upstairs and leaves me alone in a torment of confused emotions. I wish she would give me a chance to say it back, but she doesn't. I guess I've been saying it enough tonight in more ways than one.

I take myself upstairs and check in with Alvin that he's getting ready for bed, too. He is.

That leaves me to decide where I'm going to sleep tonight. I stop in the master bedroom door and stare at the bed—the bed I shared with McKenna.

Please Dear God in Heaven let me share this bed with her again. What will I do if she gives birth to the baby and dies anyway? Will I sleep on the couch for the rest of my life? Will I expect the baby to sleep down there in the living room with me?

I would have to move back into this room. I would just have to sack it up and keep living. I couldn't crumble away into oblivion.

I go downstairs, get my laptop and phone, and bring them up to the bedroom. This is my room now whether McKenna's here or not—or whether the baby is here or not. This is my life now and I'm going to live it for better or for worse.

Chapter 25: McKenna

Jackson scoops me up in his arms and carries me out of my hospital room. "You know they have wheelchairs for this, right?" I tell him.

"To hell with that. Which is more comfortable—this or a wheelchair?"

I smirk at him. "How could I say no to a hot, sexy stud like you carrying me around?"

He looks away. "I'm none of those things."

"Of course you are. You're a hunk."

"You're the only one who thinks so."

"No, I'm not. All the magazines talk about you that way. They all say you're one of the hottest guys in the country."

I make a face. "Will you stop it? Anyway, I'm engaged."

I giggle, but I have to stop talking about that when we get out to the waiting room and meet up with Alvin and Evie. "Don't they have wheelchairs for that?" Alvin asks.

Evie beams up at me. "It's romantic!"

Alvin rolls his eyes. "Yuck."

I laugh again, but Jackson pretends not to hear. "Grab your stuff, kids. We're getting the hell out of this dump."

Alvin pumps his fist. "Yes!"

They follow Jackson out of the hospital. Alvin runs ahead and opens the front passenger door of the car for Jackson to put me into the seat. It looks an awful lot like they planned this ahead of time.

The three of them buckle in and Jackson drives us back to the estate. I can't stop smiling when I look out the car window at the countryside rolling past. It feels amazing to be out of the hospital and driving through town in the sunshine.

I roll down the window and put my face near it to let the wind blow through my hair. It feels exquisite and delicious. Everything about the world feels heavenly. My life is so beautiful and full to bursting with happiness.

Jackson stretches his hand across the seat and takes mine. He doesn't interrupt my thoughts. The kids don't comment on us holding hands in front of them.

He drives one-handed and steers into the estate driveway. I drink in the sight of the sun on the fields and the mansion in the distance. He parks by the lake house and gets out to carry me inside.

"Wait a minute," I murmur. "Just let me sit here and look at it."

"I'll put a chair out on the deck for you," he tells me. "Then you can sit there and look at it all you like."

He leaves me sitting there, brings a lounge chair out to the deck, and carries me up there. He kisses me on the forehead and leaves me alone to sit and admire the view.

The sun feels magical on my face. The sound of Jackson and my children talking inside the house—it's the greatest happiness I've ever felt.

Jackson brings me a sandwich and a glass of juice in a little while. He pulls another chair over to sit next to me while we eat lunch together.

We don't speak. We just keep shooting side glances at each other and smiling.

This place—it heals the soul. He heals the soul. We're going to be a family together. I never have to worry about how he'll take care of our children and how much this means to him.

He's the best man I could ever hope to find. I knew when I met him that he was something special—and I was right. Now all my dreams are coming true.

I don't tell him my gut premonition that I'll stay healthy after I give birth. He'll find out. He would stick with me and love me every hour of every day even if he knew I wouldn't stay healthy.

This time is beyond precious—and now it's ours to share. I never could have asked for a better life than this and he's giving it to me.

He waits for me to finish and takes my dish and glass back into the house. I hear him doing things in there and then he brings his laptop and phone out to the deck to work next to me.

Everything about him anchors me to reality. He's always there, always steady, always reliable. He's everything I need and more.

He gets engrossed in his work and forgets to make eye contact with me. I find myself studying him and admiring him from the side. I admired him for years while I worked for him. I thought he was the nicest, smartest, most caring member of The Billionaires' Club.

Now I think he's a hero. He's the man who saved my family, my children, and me. He's perfect in every way—and he's mine.

No other woman has ever held his heart, shared his heart, protected his heart, and won his heart. He's all mine forever. I'll never give him up to anything except maybe death.

The sun starts to go down and he goes inside to make dinner. I relax in my seat. I'm still weak, but I'm getting better every day.

I hear Jackson telling the kids to get ready for dinner. Dishes and cutlery clink on the tabletop. He's setting out our places. I can't wait to go in there and sit down with them. The world didn't feel like the right place without being there to share that with them.

Jackson comes back out onto the deck and pulls his chair close to me. He gazes down at me from directly above. "The kids are coming down to dinner. I'm going to take you inside to eat with us."

I caress his cheek. "I love you."

"There's just one thing we need to do before dinner," he tells me.

I frown at him. "What's wrong? I feel fine."

He pulls a black velvet ring box out of his pocket, cracks it open, and shows me a magnificent diamond engagement ring. "You did say." He pulls out the ring and slips it on my finger. "Unless you suddenly changed your mind."

I pull him down and shut my eyes against his hair. I can barely whisper, "I love you."

He hugs me back and he doesn't let go. "You're mine," he breathes. "You'll always be mine."

We're still holding onto each other when Evie calls from somewhere inside the house. "Jackson! I can't find my gym shorts!"

He chuckles, pulls out of my arms, and scoops me up to carry me inside. He puts me in my chair at the table and then jogs upstairs two steps at a time to help Evie. I hear them talking in her room.

He's such a good father. I love how much my kids trust him. They obviously love him as much as he loves them. Most men have to grow into fatherhood. It just comes naturally to him because he's such a loving, sensitive man.

He comes back and goes straight to the kitchen to serve the food. I can't wait to get strong enough to start helping him around the house. I want to do all of those things.

The kids come downstairs and check themselves when they see me sitting there. I'm the outsider here. I catch both of them glancing at the ring, but they don't mention it.

Jackson brings the food over, bows his head, and says grace. Both kids say, "Amen," and he starts serving them.

They talk about what happened between Jackson, Evie, and Mrs. Partridge at the parent-teacher conference I didn't get to attend because I was in the hospital. That is the very last parent-teacher conference I'm going to miss.

"Was she trying to subtly imply that we shouldn't have done that investigation that got Mrs. Campbell fired?" Evie asks. "She made it sound like we were sticking our noses into adult business."

"I didn't get that impression," Jackson replies. "I got the impression she was a little taken aback that you kids found out something about Mrs. Campbell that Mrs. Partridge didn't know. Mrs. Partridge is supposed to be on top of everything the teachers do. It's her job to know if one of them is messing up or doing something wrong. She didn't know and she even told you kids to pull your heads in when you showed her your evidence the first time. I think she was embarrassed that you caught something she didn't—and in a way, you kids caught Mrs. Partridge with her pants down, too. She should have been quicker to pick it up."

"How could she pick it up when she wasn't in the classroom to see it?" Evie asks.

"You told me she caught Mrs. Campbell in the act of trying to pry open the cashbox. Right? You also said you and the other kids took pictures of the cashbox afterward and the hinge wasn't bent. So it sounds to me like Mrs. Partridge wasn't being as vigilant as she ought to have been and you kids showed her up. I think she's embarrassed because she has egg on her face and now all the parents in your class probably know about it just like we do. I don't think she was saying you did wrong by exposing Mrs. Campbell. I think Mrs. Partridge was trying to backpedal and make up ground with the parents by saying she recognizes that you went the extra mile and it paid off—which is what she should have been doing in the first place."

Evie cocks her head to one side. "I didn't think of that. I didn't think she did anything wrong by letting it go. She said she needed more evidence."

"Maybe she did, but the whole hinge incident should have at least raised her suspicions and then you gave her all that math data on top of it all. She should have at least been switched up enough to suspect that you might be telling the truth. *She* should have been the one to place that hidden camera—not you. I think that's what she was trying to say even if she didn't say it very well."

Evie falls silent. Jackson glances over at me like he expects me to get involved or somehow manage his handling of my daughter. I have nothing to say and nothing to add. He's acting as Evie's father—which is exactly what she needs.

It's going to become more important as the years go on that Jackson and I back each other up when it comes to the kids. If he makes a play, I'll ride with it. I won't say I disagree with him unless I do it in private. I won't second-guess him in front of the kids.

The whole conversation makes an impression on the kids. They treat him as their father now, too. They confide in him, get his opinion and input, rely on his reassurance—what could possibly be wrong with that?

They obviously need that from him. He's been their foundation the whole time I've been sick. He's the one who has been taking up the slack and doing the job I should have been doing.

I can't even feel defensive about that. I love him for it. I don't want to stand in the way of the obvious bond between them.

I don't even want to know what the three of them have been going through while I've been out of commission. They've obviously gone through the fire together and it shows.

They're closer. They're closer than close. They're family. That never could have happened if I had been here to referee the whole thing.

Jackson gets the kids to help him clear the table. Then he carries me to the living room where I can sit nearby and watch him help them with their homework.

He doesn't send them to bed at the usual time. They stop working on their homework at the usual time and then they sit up talking for another hour and a half afterward.

The same thing happens. They talk about whatever the kids have on their minds, whatever might be bothering them, or just talking about their plans for the upcoming week.

It's so heartening to see the three of them interacting like this. He's right in the middle of their lives like he belongs here. He does belong here. He's family. He's their other parent.

I would have gotten defensive before and pushed him away if someone had tried to become my children's other parent. Now I thank High Heaven that he's here. This moment offers undeniable testimony to how far they've come in the last couple of months.

The kids finally excuse themselves for bed. He doesn't send them. He waits for them to be ready to go by themselves.

He hugs them both and tells them both he loves them before they leave. They both hug him back and tell him that they love him, too. That moment seals the deal. He's family. They love him and he loves them. No one would ever guess he wasn't their biological father.

He comes back to sit down next to me while he gathers up the pieces of paper and devices they've been using to work on the kids' homework.

I rub Jackson's back. "You are so wonderful."

He barely glances at me. "They're wonderful. They're the best. It's an honor and a privilege to give them all I got."

I stroke his hair. "I am so happy and grateful to be home with you. This is the best homecoming I could have asked for."

He leans over and rests his weight on me to kiss me. He stays there extra long while our lips join. This is the most passionate we've been able to get since I first went into the hospital.

His weight on top of me feels good. He feels amazing. I don't want to let him go, but he eventually straightens up and carries me upstairs. He leaves me on the bed while he goes through the house closing the doors and turning off the lights.

I hear him checking with the kids and wishing them both good night before he comes back into the room. He goes around straightening up before he takes his clothes off, gets into bed, and switches off the light.

He wraps his arms around me and sinks back on the mattress with a shaky sigh. "I can't believe it!" he whispers. "I never thought it would happen—and now you're here! Oh, God, you feel so good!"

I can't keep away from him. I roll against his side and drape my body over him to kiss him. I kiss him deep and let the energy build between us. I missed him. I need him now. I don't want to wait any longer.

His eyes snap open to stare at me. "Don't think you're going to wear yourself out and exhaust yourself when you just came home. You're supposed to be convalescing."

I laugh at him. "How do you know I would exhaust myself? Maybe I need sexual healing."

He bursts out laughing. "Now I've heard everything."

"Come on." I squirm and undulate my body against him. "I'm frustrated. I need you."

He settles down still chuckling. "You better behave yourself."

"What—are you going to make me wait until marriage?"

He laughs again. "I should."

"Don't tell me you aren't frustrated. Don't tell me you haven't been going crazy without me."

He gazes up at me with his eyes twinkling. "I haven't, actually. I've been an absolute Boy Scout."

"Liar!" I tease.

He only smiles. "Loving you is all I need. Just loving you feels better than any sex could—loving you and being in a family with you and the kids. It's pure heaven."

I roll all the way on top of him and feel him getting hard, but I don't sit upright or fly into a frenzy. I can't. I'm not strong enough.

I straddle him and stroke my wetness down his shaft. He groans in ecstasy and glides his hands up and down my sides, back, ass, and thighs.

He angles his hips in just the right way to slip inside me, but he doesn't take it any further than that. He lies there blissfully kissing me while I stroke ever so slowly up and down his shaft. I don't have the energy to take it any further or faster than that.

Being pregnant turns me on more than I ever thought possible. I want to do it with him in all the primal frenzy we shared before. I want him to seize me, slam me down on the mattress, and take me.

He won't do that—not until I'm much stronger and we get to know each other again—but he will. We'll get there eventually because we're going to have a lot of wonderful years together.

I get tired long before anything happens. I slide off him and droop onto the mattress next to him. He only folds me in his arms and kisses my hair with a sweet smile on his face.

He doesn't tell me to rest or that we'll have all the time in the world for that. Maybe he's starting to get that gut feeling the same way I am.

Chapter 26: McKenna

"Could you please hand me that packet of bobby pins on the bed?" I ask.

Samantha Mulholland Prince pushes a bunch of different stuff back and forth on the bed. "Where is it? I don't see any bobby pins."

I turn around in my seat and point across the bedroom. "Right over there."

"It isn't on the bed because it's right in front of you on the dresser, McKenna," Piper Legrange tells me from the chair by the window. "You were using the bobby pins earlier and they're still there."

I frown at the pile of stuff in front of me. "Where? I looked, but I didn't see them."

She stands up, comes over to me, pushes some of my eyeshadow palettes out of the way, and hands me the packet. "There."

"Thanks, sweetie," I tell her. "I can never find anything anymore. I never should have let Jackson talk me into this."

"I think it's romantic," Melody Gottlieb adds from her place at the head of the bed. "I think it's a really nice gesture—you all moving up to the mansion after the wedding. This lake house can be like your honeymoon getaway. The mansion is your real house."

"It can't be their honeymoon getaway if they lived here before their wedding," Vivian Salazar chimes in from the corner by the door.

"You know what I mean," Melody counters. "It's sweet and romantic and it's a sign of new beginnings."

"It would have been great if I didn't have to pack everything right before the wedding."

"But you don't really have to," Vivian points out. "You can just come down here whenever you want and get anything you forgot to send up to the mansion before."

"I won't be able to come down here and get my veil before the ceremony." I add a few more bobby pins to hold my veil and headpiece in place. "And I need a new memory card installed, too, while we're at it. So tell the technician before he comes to troubleshoot my onboard computer."

The others laugh, and just then, Alvin sticks his head through the door. "Niko is here, Mom. He says it's time for you to go."

"I'm coming, sweetheart. I'm only way down."

I stand up and take one last look at myself in the mirror. I look like a bride in my wedding dress and veil. No one can see that I'm already pregnant with the groom's baby. I haven't started to show yet.

Vivian opens the door for me and the women help carry my train downstairs. I step out of the lake house living room onto the deck. I know I'll come back here often in the years ahead, but I won't ever call this house my home again.

Jackson, the kids, and I are moving to his old apartment in the mansion after the wedding. It has more space and extra bedrooms. We'll need that for when the baby comes.

The mansion also doesn't have any stairs I'll have to walk up and down. My strength keeps coming back the longer I stay pregnant, but I still get tired walking up and down the stairs.

Niko Holloway meets me on the deck and takes my hand. "You look stunning. Jackson is a lucky guy."

I blush at him. "Don't let him find out you were flirting with the bride."

"I'm standing right here," Melody chimes in from the back. "I can see he's keeping it clean."

Niko turns away grinning. "Come on. I don't want to keep Jackson waiting."

The women all lift my dress and train so I can walk down the steps and get into the passenger seat of Jackson's Range Rover. Niko gets behind the wheel. The women get into the back seat and Alvin gets into the farthest rear seat.

Niko drives us up to the estate and we enter through the front entrance. Niko hurries through the building to the terrace in the back.

The women flutter around me, help me arrange my skirts, and kiss me on the cheeks to congratulate me before they race away in the same direction.

Alvin is the only one left behind. He comes toward me and catches my eye. "I love you, Mom," he murmurs.

"I love you, too, sweetheart. I'm so proud of you."

I kiss him on the forehead and take his hand. He pivots sideways and places my hand inside his elbow like a real gentleman. I beam at him and we head through the house toward the terrace.

Organ music drifts through the big doors from out there. Alvin and I stop inside the atrium and exchange another glance just as the music changes to the bridal march.

He escorts me outside where our friends and families stand for the wedding. Jackson, Lane, Dante, and Derek line up on one side of the arch where the minister waits for us to join them.

Jackson has never told me why he chose those three men to be his groomsmen. He says it's personal and they were there for him while I was sick in the hospital. I don't need to know anything else. I'd rather forget that time ever happened.

Evie, Samantha, Emberlynn, and Vivian occupy the bride's side of the arch. Jackson's brothers, their wives, and some of their older children stand in the crowd along with a whole bunch of members of The Billionaires' Club, their wives, and more people from Metcalf Mining Industries.

I blush and beam at them all on my way down the aisle—until my gaze inevitably locks on Jackson. I've never been prouder to be his. We're more in love than ever and things just keep getting better with every passing day.

Alvin stops me in front of the arch. "Who gives this woman in holy matrimony?" the minister asks.

"My sister and I do," Alvin replies.

Jackson steps forward, hugs Alvin, and takes my hand from him. The other billionaires pull Alvin over to the groom's side to stand with the other groomsmen.

Alvin looks so small standing there in his tux, but he blushes with pride when they pat him on the back and tell him he did great.

Jackson's eyes go hard when he stares deep into my soul and turns me toward the arch. This is the moment we've been waiting for. We're getting married.

We'll seal our souls together for all time. We'll face challenges and hardships, but that's inevitable. Our challenges and hardships won't be any harder or more challenging than anyone else's.

The ceremony will end and life will go back to being life. We'll face all those challenges together and get through them the way everyone else does—by sticking together as a family and loving each other through it all.

Epilogue: Jackson

I come out onto the terrace and join the other members of The Billionaires' Club by the buffet. This is a casual get-together with dozens of kids running around all over the lawns behind my house.

Lane, Niko, and Judah all turn away from their conversation to shake my hand. "Is everything under control?" Judah asks.

I roll my eyes and make a face. "Apart from the main heating and ventilation system breaking down when we're a few weeks away from serious winter weather setting in? Everything is fine."

They all laugh. "You didn't think it would break down in the middle of summer, did you?" Niko asks. "That would be way too easy."

Alvin comes over to me just then and hands me a plate loaded to the gills with barbecue, four different salads, and an enormous stack of fresh, sizzling French fries.

"Here you go, Dad," he tells me. "Mom would have a conniption fit if I let you go hungry."

"Holy cow, son!" I exclaim. "What are you trying to do—give me a heart attack? I can't eat all this!"

Judah claps Alvin on both shoulders. "Look at this guy! You're almost as tall as I am. What have you been doing—working out?"

Alvin blushes. He can pretty much look Judah in the eye from the same height now. Alvin still has some inches to put on before he gets as big in the shoulders, though.

"I'm trying to catch up with Dad," he replies.

"Good luck with that," Lane tells him.

"I saw you driving around in that new Porsche of yours," Niko interrupts. "That is one sweet car, kid. Did your dad give you that for your sixteenth birthday?"

"Hell no. He bought it with his own money." Now it's my turn to clap my son on the shoulder. "You fellas are looking at a future member of The Billionaires' Club. You heard it here first."

Alvin turns bright red. "Not yet, Dad."

The shriek of childish laughter breaks out just then and we all turn to look down the lawn at the kids running around. My five-year-old daughter Gloria and my two-year-old son Ellis run around with all the other billionaires' kids.

They throw water balloons while McKenna runs after them trying to catch Ellis. His pants have slipped down past his backside and he runs with them bunching his knees together, but that doesn't stop him.

He stops to pick up one of the fallen water balloons the other kids haven't burst yet. She catches him and hikes his pants up before he realizes what's happening.

She lets him go and he runs off, but not before three other kids plaster her with water balloons and drench her hair and dress.

Me, Alvin, and the rest of the guys burst out laughing at the sight. She shoots the kids a death glare and then smirks. "I'm gonna get you for that!"

The kids scream in mock terror and run for it. She dives for a few more water balloons that lie forgotten on the grass and lobs them at the fleeing kids. She hits three of them and makes them scream again. Now it's all on.

She runs around with them throwing more balloons and taking hits from all sides. She's the only adult brave enough to go out there.

A commotion near the doors breaks out. I glance that way to see a bunch of women gather around Evie. She finally made it.

She's as tall as I am and she's grown into a beautiful, statuesque young woman of eighteen. The women make a big fuss over her and she smiles and blushes when they hug her. I don't go over there. I'll get my turn pretty soon.

"Wow," Lane breathes. "What a heartstopper."

"A heartbreaker is more like it," Alvin tells us. "She turns guys down every day."

Evie splits away from the women and comes over to hug me. "Hi, Dad," she greets me.

"Hello, sweetheart," I tell her. "I haven't seen the Bat Signal in the sky lately."

She laughs and colors. "I had to retool the Batmobile last month. It's still in the shop."

"Did you hear the news?" Judah asks the others. "Evie got into NYU for criminal justice."

"No way!" Niko exclaims. "Congratulations!"

"You're going to have your work cut out for you if you want to keep up with your sister, Alvin," Lane adds.

"Naw," Alvin replies. "I'm going to Cornell."

"For vulcanology," I chime in.

"What—did you already get admitted?"

"No, but I will," Alvin replies.

"What about your business?" Judah asks.

"What about it?" Alvin asks. "I can keep doing it while I'm in school. I'm doing it now while I'm in school. I can do both."

Lane raises his eyebrows at me, but I let it pass. I've been hearing this for the past five years. I might be tempted to intervene if Alvin wasn't killing it so badly in his business already.

He runs a real estate brokerage firm in midtown Manhattan buying and selling the most expensive luxury apartments available in the city.

Some of the biggest names in The Billionaires' Club are his clients. I would be stupid to stand in the way of that—and he never lets his grades slip, either. He really can do both.

McKenna comes up the steps just then. Water drenches her hair and clothes. Her cheeks flush with vitality and her eyes sparkle with mischief. The other guys laugh at her.

"Don't touch me until I change," she tells everyone, steals one kiss from me, and disappears inside.

We all laugh. She's never looked back or had another health crisis since Gloria was born. McKenna stays active, runs around after our kids, and she even helps me manage my companies.

The rest of us go back to our conversation. Alvin and Evie move effortlessly in this world. They've grown up in The Billionaires' Club and treat everyone here as family.

McKenna comes out of the house wearing a different dress and with her hair redone. She comes over to me, slips her arm behind my waist, and I put my arm around her shoulders while we eat and talk to our friends.

This is the life—the best life there is. It doesn't get any better than this.

<u>End of Book 7.</u>

Keep Reading

The Billionaires' Club Series: Book 8: New Blood

Everyone admires Kevin Drake for his warm, effortless interpersonal relationship and negotiating skills. He runs a mega-personnel empire, so he's perfect for the role as The Billionaires' Club's membership officer. It's his job to introduce new members to the club, show them around, and handle their applications. He immediately hits it off with new billionaire Paige Novak. She fits right into the club and starts doing business deals with everyone, including Kevin.

Paige has personal problems of her own, though. Her husband, Trent, isn't happy about her new wealth or all the rich, powerful, good-looking men at the club who now spend more time with her than he does. Things come to a head when Trent forbids her to be alone in the same room with any of her business partners, especially Kevin. She does her best to accommodate Trent's wishes, but he dumps her for no reason and proceeds to desecrate their bedroom with four other women the very next day.

With her marriage in ruins and her business launching into the stratosphere, Paige is now free to rebuild a better, more fulfilling life with someone who understands all the ups and downs her new status requires. Kevin is the answer to her prayers, but could this be the worst mistake that will bring both of their worlds crumbling down around their ears?

You can find it at your favorite book retailer.

Get All of AE Moran's Free Books

S ign Up Once—Get all A.E. Moran's free books including brand new releases

Holden Seager is hot, magnetic, and filthy, stinking, obscenely rich. He commands a room the minute he walks in the door. So what happens when meets another shark as powerful, as charismatic, and as successful as he is—not to mention ten years younger? When these two meet across the negotiating table, one of them will walk away the undisputed winner. The other will walk away with nothing.

Or so it seems.

Unless they're best friends.

When the business deal of a lifetime falls flat on its face and neither of these titans knows how to bring it back to life, this might be the opportunity Dayna Turner has been waiting for.

There's just one problem. She works as an assistant to one of these powerful men....and she's in love with the other. It's a recipe for disaster and heartbreak—unless Dayna can pull off an even bigger coup that will leave them all richer, happier, and more closely connected than ever. The alternative is the destruction of everything all three of them have worked so hard to build.

Sign up at www.authoraemoran.com to read it for free.

About AE Moran

A.E Moran is the contemporary romance pen name for Theo Mann.

I write 70 books per year—and yes, before you ask, all these books are my original creative work. Nothing written under my name is AI-generated or ghostwritten because I write better than AI and any ghostwriter out there.

People don't read fiction for entertainment or to escape from reality. People read fiction to see their humanity reflected in another person's character and story.

This is my promise to you. When you read my books, you'll see your own humanity reflected in the characters and stories. I take this commitment to my readers very seriously. My books are an intimate form of communication between us. I would never disrespect my readers by turning that over to a machine or another writer. This is my bond between me and you as my reader.

I write 20,000 words per day as my daily work output. If anyone with a public platform would like to challenge me to prove this in a controlled environment, feel free to contact me on this website's contact page.

I worked as a professional ghostwriter for fifteen years. Now I'm going for the Guinness World Record by writing 700 books over the next ten years and 1400 books over the next twenty years, all originally written by me. See my website for the full book list.

I'm also the author of *Proof for the Existence of God* and the *Crimes Against Fiction* blog. You can find all my nonfiction work at www.crimes-against-fiction.com.

If you have a story idea, or if you would like me to explore a series in more depth, or if you'd like me to explore a character by writing a spinoff series about that character or world, leave me a message on my website's contact page. I answer all reader emails, so ask me anything, tell me what you liked and didn't like, and let me know where you'd like your favorite series to go. I would love to hear your ideas and find out what you'd like to read next.

You can find out more at www.theomann.com or at www.authoraemoran.com.

Also by AE Moran (so far)